SWEET BOY
AND WILD ONE

Visit us at www.boldstrokesbooks.com

By the Author

A Class Act

Sweet Boy and Wild One

SWEET BOY AND WILD ONE

by

T.L. Hayes

2017

SWEET BOY AND WILD ONE

ISBN 13: 978-1-62639-963-1

THIS TRADE PAPERBACK ORIGINAL IS PUBLISHED BY
BOLD STROKES BOOKS, INC.
P.O. BOX 249
VALLEY FALLS, NY 12185

FIRST EDITION: AUGUST 2017

CREDITS
EDITOR: RUTH STERNGLANTZ
PRODUCTION DESIGN: SUSAN RAMUNDO
COVER DESIGN BY JEANINE HENNING

Acknowledgments

Even though the bulk of writing is done alone, either in offices, coffee shops, lovely parks, or public transportation, no book ever hits the shelf without a team of dedicated book people behind it. I just do the story writing bit, but the team at Bold Strokes Books has to do all the book making bits. Hats off to all the people working behind the scenes who literally put this book together and a special shout out to the folks in cover design who put together a beautiful cover. Also, thanks to my intrepid editor, Ruth Sternglantz. She makes me look as if I know what I'm doing.

As always, I didn't write this book on purely my own efforts. Occasionally, I had to get a little help from people who are way smarter than me and experts in their fields.

There are some medical elements to this novel that went way beyond my knowledge. Since the scenes in question required more than knowing about Band-Aids, I sought the advice of Jennifer Gusme, an x-ray and CT technician at a free-standing emergency room in San Antonio, and a US Army veteran. She was patient with all my questions (and I asked A LOT of questions) and guided me along the way to make sure my character's injuries were real. I asked her way more questions than the text indicates, I'm sure some of them tedious, but what I gained from her made for a richer section of the story. Any and all accuracies in that regard are because of her diligence and patience; any failings are entirely my own. Thanks, Goose, and thank you for your service.

Fellow writer and my unofficial life coach (unofficial because I don't pay her), April Dawn Duncan deserves much thanks for a multitude of things, only some of which have to do with this book. In that regard, I sought her advice for all things

Kung Fu. Again, all the things I got right in regard to that beautiful discipline is because of her knowledge and expertise, anything I got wrong was probably due to me being a Shăguā.

For Bobby's beautiful song, "It's About Me," a tremendous thanks goes to Abigail Zierling-Lewis and her band, Luna Lacuna. Even while planning a wedding and a million other things, she was able to create something beautiful for this book. When I asked, she didn't hesitate. Thank you so much for composing this and letting me use it. If you would like to hear the song, go here: www.lunalacuna.co.uk/Abigail

Though I did not use them for this project, I want to give a special shout out to my beta readers, the ones who read all the other things I write before I send them out. Short stories don't usually give one the opportunity to say thank you, so I will do it here: thanks to Sarah Kelley, Kristen Van Horn, Marissa Backues, Lara LaDage, Genny Maguire, Wendy Malone, and April Dawn Duncan. They always give me great feedback, even when it hurts. I thank them for being a part of my team and they are a big reason I am able to do what I do.

Many thanks to Genny Maguire for giving me a room of my own in which to write.

Dedication

For Sterling Debussy, a fine young man,
and one of the sweetest boys I know.
May you find your wild one.

CHAPTER ONE

Rachel Cole surveyed herself in the full-length mirror on the back of her dorm room door. She was in faded hip-hugger jeans, her favorite brown leather boots, and a light blue T-shirt, and over that, a blue and white flannel with the sleeves rolled up and the bottom tied taut at her waist. She thought the look was perfect for open mic night at her favorite café, which was owned by a fabulous hippie lesbian couple—Tiff and Al—who hosted something every weekend. The crowd was almost always populated with other twentysomething lesbians like herself, as well as old-school lesbians, some in granny skirts and some in leathers, there to enjoy the show or to perform. It was a great place to cruise, and it was currently Rachel's favorite weekend distraction. She hadn't had anyone to warm her bed all semester and the semester was already a month old, but she was hopeful. Sometimes she thought that since this was her last year in the grad program at Prairieland State, she should just concentrate on her studies and forget about dating. Some things were more important than sex, after all, such as getting out of Illinois and moving as far away from her parents as possible. She pulled her hair back in a ponytail, applied just a little lip gloss and her favorite scent, took one last look at herself, and let out a breath. Then she grabbed her keys and left.

Half an hour later, Rachel sat alone at a table for two, nursing a latte and wishing the café had a liquor license. It was always much easier to ask a girl out when she had a little liquid encouragement. She took a look around the room at the crowd—mostly regulars. The few new faces she saw all seemed to be coupled up except one—a hot little butch off to her left, also alone at a table for two, with earbuds in and her eyes closed and her hand keeping the beat on the table. She must be performing tonight, Rachel thought, preparing for the show.

Rachel wondered just what kind of voice that sexy creature would have. If her voice matched the rest of her, something sensual and smoky.

After listening to three performers, two of whom were angst-ridden poets Rachel hadn't cared for and one singer who had been decent, the sexy butch across the room took the stage and Rachel paid close attention. The girl grabbed a stool and adjusted the mic to her sitting position, then pushed her hat back, a blue and white check similar to Rachel's flannel, that looked as if she was wearing it askew on purpose.

Normally Rachel hated such purposeful affectation, but this girl made it work. Her jeans were ripped at the knee and she had a tank top on under her unbuttoned denim shirt, which revealed that she was flat chested. Rachel didn't mind. Boobs could be fun to play with, but it was the nipple that brought the most excitement anyway, so big boobs had never been a priority for her. This girl was hot and Rachel promised herself that she wasn't leaving the café until she had this girl's name, number, and arm around her waist.

"Evening everyone. I'm Bobby Layton. I'm going to do a little Bonnie Raitt for you tonight. It's a song called 'I Will Not Be Broken.'" Then she paused, looked down, and gave a slight nod to her right to the house band, and the music started and she began to sing. Her voice was deep and soulful, full of sorrow, yet determined.

Rachel could tell that Bobby felt every word and that she must have gone through hell but had come out of it all still fighting and still sporting a cocky grin, which Rachel was sure she often wore when she wasn't singing the blues. When the song ended, the room erupted in applause and cheers, Rachel's among them. She let out a loud whistle of appreciation. Bobby looked in her direction and smiled and nodded. Rachel inclined her head slightly indicating the empty seat at her table. Bobby's smile got bigger, and she walked through the café, stopping at Rachel's table. The applause died down as the next performer took the stage.

"You were amazing! I felt every word."

"Thank you. I'm glad. What's your name?" As Bobby asked, they both took a seat.

"Oh, sorry. My name's Rachel. And you're Bobby Layton. Why does that sound familiar?"

Flashing what Rachel was sure was a flirtatious grin, Bobby said, "Well, maybe we've met before."

"I don't think so—I would have remembered. No, something about the name itself is familiar, but I can't put my finger on it." Rachel cocked her head to the right with a curious smile.

Bobby leaned closer and spoke softly, forcing Rachel to lean in to hear. "I'll tell you a secret. Layton isn't the name I was born with—I changed it." Bobby leaned back again.

"Really? Why?"

"I just wanted to distance myself from my family. So I chose the name of someone I admire."

"And who would that be? So who was the original Bobby Layton?"

"Not was, is. He was popular before I was born. Awesome blues singer. He hasn't recorded in years though. I just identify with him." Bobby shrugged.

"So, I'm unfamiliar with his music. Sing me one of his songs."

"Sing you one?"

"Yeah. Do your namesake proud."

"I don't know if I could do it justice."

"Oh my God, are you blushing?"

"Nah. Okay, I'll tell you what, I have something more appropriate in mind. Not one of Bobby Layton's songs, but someone else's. Something just for you." Bobby winked and grinned, then started to sing an older song called "Wild One."

When it was over, Rachel leaned back in her chair with one arm draped over the back of it and looked at Bobby with a cocky grin of her own. "I don't know the song, but that seems an interesting choice for someone your age. Sounds kinda dated, don't you think? Besides, you think you can tame me, huh?"

"Not sure I would want to or should."

"Then why'd you sing that to me?" Rachel asked, in full flirting mode now.

Before Bobby could come up with a response, however, one of the owners, Al, came up and put her arm around Bobby's shoulders.

"Hey, sorry to interrupt, but Bobby, my man, I need a favor."

Bobby looked up at Al and smiled but not, Rachel noticed, the flirty grin she'd been enjoying.

"What can I do for you, Al?"

"Well, the ladies are all asking me if you're going to perform again tonight. They really want you to. Can you do this for me?"

Bobby shot Rachel a questioning look.

Rachel cocked an eyebrow. "Go ahead—I'm not going anywhere."

Al patted Bobby on the back. "See, she's not leaving. What's one more song?"

"I only prepared the one song."

"Sing a Bobby Layton song," Rachel said, somewhat mischievously.

"Oh, I like that," Al agreed. "I'm sure we have women in here tonight who would love it. Come on."

Bobby sighed and looked apologetically at Rachel. "Okay. I'll be right back."

"I'll be here."

Bobby smiled at her before taking the stage amidst more applause and whistles. Bobby didn't grab a stool this time, just took the mic off the stand, turned around and whispered to the band, and then turned back around to speak to the audience. "All right, I'm going to do something a little different than I did last time. Some of you are cool enough to know the original Bobby Layton and so I'm gonna do one of his songs now."

Bobby definitely had Rachel's attention and she couldn't take her eyes off her as she moved across the stage with ease. Every so often Bobby's gaze would find Rachel and Rachel would catch a wink she was sure was meant only for her. She felt like a total fangirl and told herself to calm down.

When the song ended, Bobby bowed and said, "Thank you ladies," then threw a kiss out into the audience.

As Bobby left the stage and made his way back to Rachel, Al took the stage and said, "Bobby Layton, ladies and gentlemen—give him a hand."

The audience obliged, except for Rachel, who stopped clapping, confused. Did Al just refer to Bobby as *him*? Or did she just mishear amidst the applause?

When Bobby came back to their table she took a closer look to see if she could see anything different than she did before, though she wasn't sure what that would be.

Bobby made no move to sit. "So..."

"You're a guy?"

"Yeah." He said cautiously, as he stood there with his hands in his pants pockets, casually waiting for her response.

Rachel nodded. "My bad, I thought you were a girl. I think my gaydar's broken or something." Then she laughed somewhat nervously.

"It's okay, happens all the time. I'm trans." His expression showed nothing and she wasn't sure how he felt about her mistaking his gender.

"I see. So that's why you changed your name."

"Partly. I also really did want to distance myself from my family. My parents aren't exactly cool with all this."

"Uh-huh." Rachel leaned back in her seat, almost in a daze, not sure what to say.

Bobby sat finally, a look of concern marring his features. "Are you okay?"

Shaking her head, Rachel said, "Yeah, sorry. Didn't mean to freak out." She tried to smile as she sat up straighter and no longer leaned away from him.

"It's okay, I'm getting used to it. You're not the first person to react this way and I'm sure you won't be the last."

"Sorry. But this doesn't mean we can't be friends." Rachel attempted a smile.

Bobby chuckled derisively. "Friends?" He suddenly sounded bitter and angry. "Yeah, cause that's totally why you invited me to your table, to be *friends*. And this is why I don't date lesbians." Abruptly, Bobby stood up from the table, knocking his chair back in the process as he stormed out the front door.

Under her breath, Rachel said, "Wow, what an ass." As she said it however, she wasn't sure if she was referring to him or herself.

❖

Rachel left the café shortly thereafter, still uncertain about everything. She had really liked Bobby, thought he was hot when she thought he was a dyke. So why was it different now, she wondered? *Because I'm not into dudes, it's just that simple*, she thought. Rachel knew eventually he would lose the roundness in his face and his body would square off and lose its softness—all the things she found attractive. Should she feel guilty for only being attracted to women? It was something she had known and accepted about herself since high school.

So why do I feel guilty? She had just never been attracted to men, period. Butch lesbians, sure, but that was different. Underneath the boy clothes and the short hair was still the softness and curves of a woman. There was just nothing about the male body that appealed to her. She couldn't explain the laws of attraction any better than anyone else could; she just knew what she liked, not why.

Coupled with that was his overreaction to her comment about being friends. It was totally uncalled for and showed him to be a jerk. He sounded bitter and angry about something that really had nothing to do with her, and though she didn't know what he had gone through with other lesbians to warrant that kind of attitude, she didn't deserve to take the heat for whoever might have treated him badly in the past. She just didn't need that kind of bullshit in her life.

Focusing on his negative attitude helped some to relieve the guilt she felt.

As she turned into the parking lot next to her dorm, she scanned the lot looking for an open spot as close to the door of the building as she could get. Finding a spot three rows away from the front door, she parked and got out. It was too bad, really. Bobby had been really hot. *Too bad he's an asshole*, she thought.

As she made her way up to her room, she worked on putting her game face back on. By the time the elevator opened on her floor, her smile was in place and she walked with a self-assurance she did not feel. She and Rory, her best friend who'd moved to Minnesota over the summer after falling in love with one of their professors and causing a minor campus scandal, used to refer to walking down the hallway after a night out as walking the gauntlet, since there were bound to be other people milling about, looking on in judgment.

Sure enough, just as she passed Rory's old room, the door next to it opened and Lori popped her head out her door. Lori was someone she sometimes hung out with and slept with when the mood struck her, though they hadn't hooked up in months. Lori had started to become clingy and possessive and hadn't been able to handle just keeping things casual. When Rachel told her she didn't want to continue sleeping with her anymore, Lori took it hard for a while but she seemed to have gotten over it and they had worked their way into a tolerable friendship.

"Rach, you're home early."

Rachel stopped to chat, making sure the smile was firmly in place. "Yeah, slim pickings tonight. Everyone was already coupled up. No single ladies." She said the last in the style of Beyoncé and Lori smiled.

"I see why you left early. Come in, Molly and Lanie are here—I made Jell-O." Lori's eyes danced mischievously and probably a bit drunkenly, Rachel thought.

"I don't like Jell-O."

"Everyone likes Jell-O shots, silly." Lori tugged on her arm.

"Jell-O shots? Why didn't you say so? There's always room for Jell-O shots." Rachel allowed herself to be pulled into the room with the other girls. She knew if she played her cards right, she could have Lori sleeping in her bed before the night was over, but she also knew she didn't want to go down that road again. She wasn't that desperate. Maybe she would just drink a few shots and go back to her room, alone.

CHAPTER TWO

On Saturday, Rachel decided to stay in and once again found herself in Lori's room. Tonight, it was Jagerbombs. Not Rachel's favorite at all—she hated both components of the drink. She politely declined, preferring just soda for once. She let the chatter surround her head like a dense fog. When one of the girls, Molly, she thought, suggested pizza, she came alert enough to put her two cents worth in the vote for toppings.

It was agreed they would order from the place closest to campus and Rachel zoned out again. She had thought about calling Rory earlier in the day, but to say what? *Yeah, I made an ass of myself in front of this person I think is really hot, even if he is kind of a jerk and he probably hates me now. How was your day?* But she'd decided against it. She wasn't sure how to explain the fact that she might be attracted to a guy.

When the knock came a half hour later, Rachel was the one sitting closest to the door, so she answered it. For a moment, she thought her mind was playing tricks on her. Then she remembered that she was stone-cold sober. Standing in front of her, with a leather warming bag in one hand and a receipt in the other, was Bobby, still as hot as he had been the night before, the red and black uniform not distracting from his attractiveness at all.

Rachel couldn't speak for a moment and it looked like Bobby was surprised as well, but he recovered first.

"Hi—I got one pepperoni and sausage and one cheese, medium. That'll be $25.84."

"Oh, yeah, here." Rachel pulled out her wallet from her back pocket and called, "I got this, guys," to the group over her shoulder, which had all gone silent staring at Bobby. She handed him two bills and said, "Keep the change."

Bobby's face was unreadable. "Thanks." He took the money from Rachel's hand and handed her the pizza. "Actually, I'll give up my tip if you give me your number instead." Bobby grinned and the girls behind Rachel could barely contain themselves.

"Seriously? You didn't just *seriously* ask me for my number?"

"Yeah, I did. I probably should have led with the apology first, dammit." Bobby looked away from her.

"Hold that thought." She turned and set the boxes on the chair she had been sitting on, then stepped back into the hallway, ignoring the looks from the other girls, and closed the door behind her, positive her friends would immediately go quiet so that they could eavesdrop. "Okay, apology time."

"I was kind of a jerk to you and I'm sorry."

"*Kind of* a jerk? You were *kind of* an asshole, actually. I liked you and I didn't deserve that." She crossed her arms in front of her chest defiantly.

Bobby looked down at his shoes again. "I know. I would like the chance to make it up to you."

Rachel sighed. "I don't know. I mean, putting your rudeness aside for the moment, there's also the fact—as you obviously know—I'm a lesbian. That's the only reason I backed off flirting with you. Not because of some bullshit anti-trans thing or whatever you're thinking. I just don't date guys, whether they were assigned that way at birth or not. I'm sorry."

"Look, I'm not asking you to change your identity, just your mind."

"And forgive you for putting me in the category of all the bitchy lesbians you know?"

"Yeah."

"That's a lot to ask."

"I know."

Rachel ran her hands through her hair and sighed. "Dammit to hell."

Bobby grinned.

"Don't look so confident. I'm not giving you my number because I'm suddenly straight or because I suddenly forgive you."

"Then why *are* you giving me your number?"

"I never said I was."

"But you're thinking about it." The playful smile never left Bobby's face.

"You think you're charming, don't you?"

"Baby, I know I'm charming."

"Oh my God! You are fucking exasperating is what you are." Rachel rolled her eyes.

"That's one of my better qualities."

"Does this charm thing you're trying to do actually work? I mean, are girls actually impressed by this?" Rachel asked.

"I'll let you know."

Neither one said anything for a moment. Finally, Bobby set the warming bag down and held the receipt against the wall and proceeded to write something down. As he wrote he said, "I'll tell you what. I'll give you my number and if you think you can forgive me and might want to just get to know me better and see what happens, you can call me. It'll all be up to you."

He stood back from the door and handed Rachel the receipt. With a smile, she reached for it but at the last second, he folded his fingers, moving the paper out of her reach. He wasn't as tall as Rory but he was still taller than her.

"You gonna call me?"

"Maybe. I haven't decided if I want to forgive you yet."
With a quick move, Rachel jumped and snatched the paper from
his hand, then opened the door and ducked back into the room.
She wasn't sure what was worse, the cocky grin on his face or
the questions she knew the girls were going to ask.

❖

As Rachel had expected, the girls in the room wanted all the
details, and the questions started as soon as the door closed and
came in rapid-fire succession.

"How do you know her?" Lori asked.

"Him," Rachel stated.

"She's gorgeous," Molly gushed.

"His name is Bobby."

"Did she just ask you out?" Lori again.

"He kinda did."

"Wait, why do you keep saying *he*?" Lainie asked.

"Because he's a guy."

"What? Really? No way!" Molly again.

"Yes, he's trans." Rachel regretted saying it as soon as it
was out of her mouth.

"And he just asked you out? What'd you say?" Molly
seemed almost overeager for details.

"Well, I—"

"What do you think she said? She said no. She doesn't date
guys," said Lori, with her arms crossed over her chest.

"That's true," Molly agreed. "Too bad, he was sexy though.
Did you see those eyes? Gorgeous."

"Molly!"

Molly sulked.

"Wait, so he's only cute when you think he's a she?" Rachel
demanded. "Are you saying his gender determines his hotness? I
don't get that, please explain that to me." Rachel was starting to

get annoyed, though she wasn't sure why. They weren't acting any worse than she had the night she'd met Bobby. *Maybe I'm mad at them because I still feel guilty for the way I acted.* Geez, paging Dr. Freud.

"Well, you know, he's a guy…You should know by now what the definition of lesbian is." Lori stood over Rachel, still with her arms crossed, as if she was challenging Rachel to defy her logic.

Rachel stood up and faced her. Lori might have had her in height by a couple of inches, most people did, but Rachel knew she could be more intimidating. "Since when does the definition of lesbian include narrow-minded and prejudiced?"

"You sound like you're considering going out with him. That's quite a surprise. The Rachel I know only dates, or fucks, girls." Lori sneered at her.

"Lori, don't think just because I've fucked you that you know me. You don't know shit."

"Obviously. So, what are you saying, are you bi now or something?"

"No. I'm still the same person I always was."

"Are you sure about that?"

"Fuck you, Lori. Actually, unfuck you. I *really* wish that were possible." With that, she slammed out of the room and went back to her own. She was pissed at how the whole confrontation with Lori had gone down. She needed her best friend.

It was still kind of early, not even ten, so she didn't worry that she would be bothering Rory. Since Rory was so far away, a phone call was the best she could manage. Before she had left, Rory had told her that she could call whenever she wanted, and if she wasn't busy, she would always answer. So hoping Rory and Maggie weren't on a date or something, Rachel hit speed dial.

"Hey, how's my BFF?" Rory asked.

Rachel was amused. "Since when do you use current slang?"

"You're right, it's not me, is it?" There was the usual humor in Rory's voice and it put Rachel at her ease.

"No. Just go back to being outdated. I like you better that way."

"Fine. Being trendy is too much work anyway."

"That's why I ignore trends and just do me. So, am I interrupting anything?" Rachel asked sincerely, but hoping Rory would say no.

"No, I can take care of Maggie and talk to you at the same time." Rory snickered.

"I don't know whether to be grossed out, offended on her behalf, or impressed."

This time Rory laughed out loud. "Get your mind out of the gutter. I just meant that she has the flu."

"You jerk. You did that on purpose."

"I would never. So, why'd you call, anyway?"

Rachel told her about how she had been attracted to Bobby when she thought he was a girl, but then made an ass of herself after she found out the truth, him being a major jerk, then the accidental meeting over pizza and how he had apologized and given her his number. She told her about the girls' reactions and her response to them. Rory listened to it all, only muttering assurances that she was still listening.

"Okay. That's why I called."

"Rachel—screw them." Rory sounded indignant. "If you like him, nothing else matters. Maybe ask him why he reacted that way to you. I'm not trying to excuse him, but there's bound to be a reason."

"Yeah, but putting that aside for the moment, I'm not bi or pansexual or any other new term. I'm just plain old boring gay. I can't pretend I'm not."

"Did he ask you to?"

"Well, no. But it wouldn't be right."

"In what way?"

"In a lot of ways, but Rory, think about this. The more he starts to look like a guy I'm probably not going to think he's so cute or want to date him. I know that makes me shallow and small-minded, but that's just how it is. Like I told him, it's not an anti-trans thing, I just don't date men, period."

"Well, let me ask you this. Rachel, do you like him?"

Rachel sighed. "It all comes back to that, doesn't it?"

"Yes, it does. That's the only thing you *should* think about."

"Yes, but, what if it'd been you instead of me? Would you have gone out with him?"

Rory took a moment before she responded. Then, "I know the right thing to say is yes, but to be honest, I can't say for sure. I understand where you're coming from, I do. I mean, I want to be the type of person who says I would only date someone I truly connected with and their body and their label wouldn't matter. I wish I could say that, but that's just not me and it doesn't have to be you either. Attraction should not be based on political correctness. That being said, you just gotta go with your gut on this one. I wish I had a better answer for you."

Rachel sighed. "No, that makes sense. Let me think on it some more."

"I'm sorry I don't have better advice than that. Just don't take too long. The hot ones get snatched up quickly."

"Oh, like you're an expert. I'm sure Maggie would have waited for you, had you foolishly been dating someone else."

"You're assuming I'm the hot one in this relationship. Rachel, I'm attractive...but Maggie's gorgeous."

A silence fell between them.

Finally, Rachel broke it. "I'll take your word for it. Thank you—thank you for answering."

"Anytime. Just relax, think it through, and don't worry about living up to anyone else's expectations."

"I know. I guess I should let you get back to Maggie now."

"Yeah. The doc needs some doctoring and much TLC. Keep me posted."

"I will."

CHAPTER THREE

So after having spent the night thinking it over, Rachel decided to give Bobby a call. But not before she got up, brushed her teeth and her wild hair, and made sure her voice didn't sound sleepy. She hadn't actually read what he had written the night before. Now she smiled as she studied the receipt. *Call me, Wild One. I promise, I won't try to tame you.*

Rachel laughed and shook her head. "You are such a dork. What the hell." She took her phone off her desk and dialed the number written on the receipt.

"Hello?"

"So, is Wild One my nickname now, or something? Cause if so, I need to know so that I can live up to it."

Bobby chuckled. "Good morning, Rachel. And who says you haven't already?"

"Really? What have I done that's so wild?"

"Well, you called me, for one."

"And that makes me wild?" Rachel asked, somewhat incredulously.

"It might to some people. Like your friends," Bobby said quietly.

"Fuck 'em. They don't make my decisions for me. If I want to get to know you better and see what happens, that's my business."

"Fair enough. So does this mean that you forgive me?" Bobby asked sincerely.

"That depends."

"On what?"

"On whether or not you will judge me based on how other girls have treated you. I'm not an asshole to people—at least, I try not to be. I may be wild sometimes, as you claim, and I have been told I don't have a filter, whatever the fuck that means, but I do my best to treat people with respect. Now I will get off my soapbox long enough to say, if you can take me as I am, I will do the same for you. I want to hang out with you today. I don't know if I'm ready to call it a date or not, but pick me up and we'll see what happens. Fair enough?"

"Yeah, more than fair."

"Good. Now get over here."

Chuckling, Bobby said, "Yes ma'am."

They decided to take a walk together and the place they chose was the campus lake, though it was more like a pond, really. It was a lovely setting, surrounded as it was by trees, the occasional bench, hills, and about two dozen ducks, who were currently eyeing Rachel and Bobby to see if they had any food to offer. When the humans made no attempt to offer them anything, the ducks went away disappointed.

Rachel was amused that they were dressed similarly in jeans and flannel, owing much to the fall weather. Bobby walked with his hands behind his back, as if he didn't have a care in the world.

"You know if you're curious, you can ask me things. If you're worried about getting too personal, don't. If I don't want to answer, I'll say so."

"Okay. There is something I've been wondering."

"Okay."

"Why...why pick some guy no one remembers as your idol?"

Bobby laughed. "That's what you want to ask me?"

"Yeah. I mean, what's the appeal?"

"Well, I like his songs. And you're right, no one remembers him and I think that's sad. Heck, he's not even dead."

"Do you write your own songs?"

"Yeah. I haven't sung them in public in a while though."

"Why not?"

"Ah, you know how it is." Bobby unclasped his hands and let them fall loosely at his sides as he kicked at a clump of dirt.

Rachel thought he was suddenly shy and she found it adorable. "No, I don't know. Maybe the real question is, do you want to spend the rest of your life singing someone else's songs and living with someone else's name, or do you want to make a name for yourself singing your own songs?" She brushed a strand of hair which had fallen in her eyes away from her face.

"Wow, the questions you ask, Rachel Cole."

"Wow, the questions you evade, Bobby Layton."

Bobby laughed. "Touché. I *do* want to sing my own songs. What, you don't like my name?"

"Oh, I think it's fine and I have no business telling you to change it. I was just making the point that if you're going to be a man, be your own man."

"You pull no punches, I'll give you that. Don't you have any questions about my transition?"

On impulse, Rachel grabbed his hand. He looked at their clasped hands and smiled but didn't say anything. "I had considered it, but I figured that's probably all you've talked about lately. Thought you might like a change of pace."

"I suppose that's true. People seem to forget I have other interests."

"So, tell me about some of your other interests."

Bobby stopped walking and looked into Rachel's eyes. "I'm interested in you."

Rachel smiled. "Well of course, that goes without saying."

Bobby laughed, then leaned down and very gently kissed her on the lips. Then he stepped back to look at her face. "You okay?"

She wasn't sure what she expected kissing him to be like. She had no frame of reference for kissing a guy. She supposed it was a good thing that his face wasn't scratchy with beard stubble. All in all though, it was just a nice, sweet kiss. "You have nice lips, Bobby Layton."

"Thank you, Rachel, so do you. Can I kiss you again?"

She surprised herself by saying, "Yes."

Instead of kissing her, however, he stepped away. "Good. Maybe later."

"You're a dork, but you're also a very sweet boy."

"Does this mean you forgive me?"

"Don't know yet." On impulse, Rachel dropped his hand and put her arms around his waist. She suddenly wanted to feel him next to her. He seemed somewhat surprised but obliged by putting both arms around her waist as well. Rachel put one hand on his chest and felt the flatness but felt something else also. "How many shirts are you wearing?"

"Under the flannel I have a T-shirt, a compression shirt, and a bra."

"Compression? Does it hurt?"

"Sometimes. Especially if I wear it longer than I should, which is most of the time." He gave a lopsided smile, then brushed a strand of hair off Rachel's cheek.

"Why do you do it?"

"Because I don't want to be a guy with tits. And it'll be a while before I can afford the surgery."

"You mean a double mastectomy, don't you?"

"Yeah."

She threw her arms around him and hugged him. He returned her hug and buried his face in her hair. She wasn't sure why she was suddenly getting emotional, but she knew she hated what he must have to go through to feel comfortable in his own skin. After a moment, she pulled away and said, "Come on Sweet Boy, I'm hungry."

❖

"So, how'd it go?"

After Bobby dropped Rachel off at her dorm with a nice, long, slow, sensual kiss, she called Rory. Rory asked her question before Rachel could get out anything more than hello.

"How'd you know I went out with him?"

"Because I know you." Rachel could hear the humor in Rory's voice and could picture the grin on her face.

"What do you mean by that?"

Rory chuckled. "I know you like him and when you like someone you don't give up."

"That makes me sound like a hunter hunting my prey."

"If the Day-Glo orange vest fits."

"See, I could never be a hunter. I could never wear something as horrid as Day-Glo orange or camouflage."

"That's true. So, give me all the details," Rory asked, sounding amused.

"Ugh, now you sound just like the girls down the hall."

"Do I? My apologies. I guess I've been hanging around you too long."

"Do you want to hear this story or not?"

Chuckling, Rory said, "I'm sorry, go on."

"Thank you. Okay, anyway, first off, I gotta say, after giving him a second chance I can say that he is actually one of the sweetest people I've ever gone out with, but also a big dork." Rachel immediately felt like she was gushing but couldn't help it and really didn't want to stop.

"So you have a lot in common."

"Aww, you think I'm sweet. Now stop interrupting." Rachel told Rory all about the date, concluding with the kiss.

"You left out the best part."

"No, I told you all the juicy details."

"You didn't mention if you're going to see him again."

"Oh, that. I'm not sure yet."

"After all that, you're not sure? How can you not be sure?"

At the moment, Rachel wished that she had been born earlier because she really wanted a phone cord to twirl around her fingers right about now. It was hard to show nervous agitation when talking on a cell phone. She settled for twirling a pen from one finger to the other with her free hand. Somehow, hemming and hawing was easier when you had something to do with your hands.

"Come on, Rachel, you can tell me. No judgment here, I hope you know that."

"I do." Rachel sighed. "Okay, here it is. I just don't know if I'm up to this. Do you know the life he has in front of him?"

"Do you?"

"I'm beginning to. He told me he has to be on hormone shots for the rest of his life. Plus, he could wait for years to have the surgeries he needs because insurance won't pay. In the meantime, he has to be physically uncomfortable because of all the crap he has to wear just to feel comfortable in his own skin. To say nothing of stupid people like me mistaking his gender."

"First of all, you're not stupid, you made an honest mistake. The fact that he still wants to go out with you means that it didn't bother him, so don't beat yourself up over it. The really stupid people are the ones who deliberately call him and others by the wrong gender."

"People are assholes."

"Not all, but a fair amount," Rory said reasonably.

"So how do you know so much about it, anyway?"

"There's a social justice group I've become involved with up here. I've met a lot of great people. Several of them are trans. I've learned a lot. And you're right about his road ahead—it won't be easy. He'll need a good support system behind him."

"Yeah, and I just don't know if I'm strong enough." Rachel sulked.

"Why do you think you're not strong enough?"

"Rory, I couldn't handle the thought of all he goes through just to flatten his chest. How am I supposed to handle everything else?" By now Rachel was pacing back and forth.

"Well, I do commend your caution. The last thing he's going to need is someone who flakes out on him."

"I know."

"But, that being said, you'd be surprised what you can handle when you care about someone."

"That sounds almost like a Christian platitude. That's not like you."

Rory laughed. "Okay fine. How about this—get your shit together and don't make that sweet boy wait too long before you let him know either way."

"Now see, that's advice I can use."

"I meant it about no judgment. Just don't be an ass."

"Okay, that's enough practical wisdom for one day," Rachel said matter-of-factly.

"Good luck."

"Thank you."

CHAPTER FOUR

Monday arrived, and Rachel hadn't called Bobby but she'd texted him a few times in response to his inquires—whether or not she was okay, and when she wanted to get together again. She had put him off with a vague reply about having a lot of work to do and she would get back to him, which she was sure he saw through, but he didn't push the issue, for which she was grateful. But she couldn't help it. She didn't know what to do. She liked him but did she like him enough to go on his journey with him? Did she like him enough to allow others to make assumptions about her identity? It was bad enough that as a femme lesbian people already thought she was straight. If she was on Bobby's arm it would be a constant fight to keep her identity in place against an ignorant, narrow-minded society who thought their view was the only right and true one.

Monday afternoon Rachel walked into her stage combat class, the one she and Rory had been planning to take together, barely there, her mind full of thoughts of Bobby. The stage combat class was her favorite class, and she was discovering that she really liked sword fighting and the artful dance that was the well-choreographed fight scene.

Class was held in one of the multipurpose rooms in the theater building, as most days they didn't need desks, just open space for sparring. They had met the first day in the same classroom in which Rory had met Maggie, which was fitting, considering that the class was taught by Maggie's replacement, Dr. Louise Silver. Dr. Silver was quickly becoming Rachel's favorite professor, though not in the same way Maggie had become Rory's. Not because she wasn't attractive, she was. Rachel had always been a sucker for curls, and Dr. Silver had a head full of honey blond ones. But she just didn't go for older women. She did, however, adore Dr. Silver for a reason that had nothing to do with her looks. She was a total badass and knew what she was talking about. Plus, she was funny.

On the first day of class she had said, "Hello, everyone. I'm Dr. Silver and I'm your new Defense Against the Dark Arts professor." The class had laughed appreciatively. Dr. Silver ruffled through the papers she had brought, pretending to look confused. "Wait, is that right? Am I in the wrong class?"

Rachel had muttered, "Great, she's probably a Death Eater or something." Some of her classmates chuckled.

Dr. Silver cocked her head and grinned. "I prefer to think I'm closer to Professor McGonagall than one of those, but I guess only time will tell, won't it?"

Rachel liked that she could joke around with her professor—so many of her professors seemed to be more on the conservative side, and joking was not something they did. Plus, her referencing Harry Potter proved to Rachel that she was probably a big geek, and though she wasn't one herself, Rachel could appreciate geekiness. Rory was kind of a geek and was often making references to geeky things that Rachel knew nothing about.

Now, with the fifth week of class starting, Dr. Silver was teaching Rachel and the rest of the class how to be just as badass as she was. Or, at least, that was Rachel's goal. She knew Dr. Silver knew her way around a sword and was confident the woman could hold her own in a fight—a real one, not just onstage—even though she didn't look the part of a fierce warrior.

She looked like the academic she usually was. She wasn't much taller than Rachel, maybe five-foot-six or so, with dark blond curls that went every which way if she didn't batten them down during class. And when she referenced something geeky, which she often did, her face danced with such delight, it was just hard to believe she was capable of kicking anyone's ass.

Dr. Silver had suggested to the class that they study types of movement in their spare time that she wouldn't be covering during the semester, but that might be beneficial to their stage-fighting toolkits. All her recommendations were activities that involved coordination and flexibility, such as dancing, rock climbing, yoga, and martial arts.

Dr. Silver practiced a style of kung fu known as Wushu and had shown the class some videos of herself and others doing some of the movements. Rachel thought it looked lovely and more like dancing instead of fighting, it was so elegant. What really captivated her, however, was the fierce look on Dr. Silver's face during her routines. Though her body was doing delicate things, her face was set in a determination that said, *Don't fuck with me*. That's the kind of badass Rachel wanted to be.

But all that being said, she wasn't sure how these extracurricular activities would help with stage combat.

"Sensei, why should we learn this?"

Dr. Silver gave her the biggest of grins. "If you are going to use martial arts terminology to refer to me, please be sure to use the correct one. What you want to say is *sifu*. And to answer your question, Rachel, because it will teach you to be light on your feet. Plus, it's just a really cool thing to know." Dr. Silver cocked her head to the side, almost in a way that invited a challenge, but Rachel knew better.

"Just to be clear, did you say *sure food*? Cause that sounds more like a grocery store than a term of respect."

"Close, Shǎguā, but drop the *d*."

"What did you call me?"

"Shǎguā. It's a Mandarin term. Look it up." The grin never wavered from Dr. Silver's face as she walked away from Rachel, who could only stand there looking puzzled.

"Mandarin? Geez, how many languages do you know?"

Dr. Silver turned and gave her a look she couldn't read. All she said was, "Enough," then turned back to the class. Rachel wasn't sure if Dr. Silver was answering her question or admonishing her.

When Dr. Silver had her back turned, Rachel quickly pulled out her phone and typed a phonetic spelling of the word she had been called into the internet search bar but nothing came up in the search. "Hey, Dr. Silver, how can I look it up if I don't know how to spell it?"

Dr. Silver turned around with an amused sigh. "Ah, the question students have asked throughout the ages. How'd you spell it?" Rachel turned her phone around and showed her the screen. "Ah, I see what you did there. You have to put U in there."

"Why do I get the feeling you're insulting me?"

"Rachel, I am a respected professor and well thought of in my field. I would never insult my students, all of whom I have nothing but respect for." Then she winked.

Just as Dr. Silver was walking away, Rachel found the proper spelling of the word and cried out, "Hey! That wasn't nice!" Yet she couldn't help but be amused. She had been acting silly and figured she kind of deserved the insult.

With her ever-present grin, Dr. Silver faced Rachel and bowed and said something else in Chinese.

"Apology accepted."

"You knew that one, huh?"

"Figured it out."

"Good show, Rachel, good show. Now can I get back to the rest of class?"

"Go ahead, don't let me stop you."

"Thank you."

They shared a smile as Dr. Silver walked away. Rachel's thoughts briefly returned to Bobby again and she realized that she should stop avoiding him and just call or text him. She really had had a good time with him and he was a really good kisser. *Dr. Silver's right. I am a simpleton.* Even though she knew she should be paying attention to what Dr. Silver was saying, something about a war fan, whatever that was, she couldn't wait any longer. She pulled her phone back out and texted Bobby. *I'm sorry I've been unavailable the last couple of days. Forgive me? Can we get together one day this week?*

The reply took several minutes. Just when Rachel was about to give up and put the phone back in her pocket, her phone vibrated and the notice appeared on her home screen that Bobby had replied. *Forgiven. I understand you're busy. I don't expect or need constant contact. Yes. When?*

Rachel could feel the grin on her face she couldn't suppress. She replied, *I have no classes tomorrow. Are you busy then?*

I have to work tomorrow night at six but I am free until then. What do you want to do?

Fast forward through the twenty minutes where we ask that question back and forth and get to the part where I just say I want to hang out with you. Talk. Ask you more embarrassing questions.

LOL. Okay. How's one or so?

Perfect.

"Rachel?"

Rachel jerked her head up at the sound of her name and quickly put her phone in her pocket before she tuned back in to Dr. Silver trying to get her attention. "Yes? What?"

"I know for a fact that this class costs more than your cell phone plan, so one would think you would want to be in this moment, with the rest of us, instead of with whoever is on the other end of that conversation. I am requesting your attention for another thirty minutes, at least."

"Sorry Dr. Silver. Won't happen again."
"Good."

❖

Bobby had shown up at her dorm an hour ago, and now Rachel was lounging with her back against her headboard, her knees drawn up to her chest. Bobby was lying at the end of the bed, in the far corner, looking at her with a mysterious smile on his face.

"Why are you looking at me like that?"

The smile didn't waver when he said, "No reason," and just shook his head.

"I think I know what that smile means."

"Do you?"

"Yeah, I think so."

"What's it mean?"

"I think you're thinking about the fact that I let you on my bed and you're wondering just how much more I'll let you get away with." She flashed him a smile of her own.

"No, I wasn't thinking that."

"Okay, then what were you thinking?"

"I see the embarrassing questions portion of the day has started." Bobby shifted and readjusted himself in the corner. His movement made Rachel laugh.

"Well, how embarrassing could it be if you weren't thinking of taking advantage of me? And why weren't you thinking of taking advantage of me?"

"Too early for that." Bobby didn't sound like he was teasing. "I mean, early in the sense of knowing you." Bobby shrugged.

"Aww." They shared a smile. Rachel extended her legs and poked him in the knee with her toes, which was the only part of her body she could reach with if she didn't want to change position, and she didn't, and asked, "So, seriously, what's going through that head of yours?"

"Nothing, really—I'm just glad you texted, Rachel. I was wondering if you would. I mean, like I said, I'm not the type of guy who needs to talk to you every day or who gets worried if it takes all day for a text back. But I know you've had your issues with me and I respect that too." This time, Bobby gave her a soft smile and put his hand on top of her denim-clad leg.

"It's not so much that I have issues with you, but I'd be an idiot if I let some bullshit label stand in the way of getting to know you better."

"And your friends?"

"What about them?"

"I got the impression they were, at the very least, fascinated by me, and at the most, probably nosy as hell."

Rachel laughed. "Yeah, that's putting it mildly. As I said before, I don't care what those nosy wenches think. They don't control what I do and they're not really my friends. They're just people I get bored enough to hang out with sometimes. I really only have one true friend and she and her future wife moved away over the summer. And I know they support me and have my back."

Bobby looked concerned. "So you're alone here, then?"

"Well, in a way, but Rory, that's my best friend, she and I talk a lot. That's your heads-up, by the way. If you're going to be a part of my life, you have to know how much she and I talk."

"She sounds very important to you."

"She is. She's awesome. I hope you get to meet her. She's a big reason why I called you in the first place, you know?"

"Really?"

"Yeah. She told me to stop being an ass."

Bobby laughed. "She sounds very wise."

"She is."

"And you love her very much." Bobby looked at her askance.

"Yeah, like I said, she's my best friend. I mean, she's definitely someone I could see myself dating—we've always had a great connection. But that kind of relationship was just not in the cards for us and that's okay." Rachel shrugged, looking almost wistful.

"Rachel, it's okay if it's more than that. Well, not okay in the sense that I want to compete with her, I mean, just okay in the sense of, I understand."

"I think you mean that."

"I do. I just try to take people for who they are and not expect them to be something they're not. That just leads to disappointment when you realize people aren't who you thought they were." He shrugged.

"You're like Zen or something. Do you meditate?"

Bobby gave a surprised laugh. "I do, actually, but I've also spent too much time wishing people were different. One day I just realized that I need to accept them for who they are—once I know who that is—and make a quick decision if who they are is someone I want to know or not. There's very little about a person I can't tolerate."

"So what can't you tolerate?" Rachel asked.

"You know, the big stuff—violence, bigotry, racism, hatred, sexism, homophobia. That kind of thing."

"But those aren't personality traits, those are beliefs or behaviors."

"Exactly. Why should I care if a roommate doesn't always do all their dishes or leaves their socks on the living room floor if they're nice to old people and puppies?"

Rachel laughed. "Old people and puppies?"

"Yes. Let the little shit go and concentrate on what really matters."

"I think I get it." They said nothing for a moment, and then Rachel cocked her head to the left and said, "Bobby, come here."

Bobby said nothing. He just slowly climbed on top of her, putting one hand on either side of her, and reached up before she could say another word and kissed her softly on the lips.

Rachel put her arms around his neck and scooted down lower so she was now underneath him. "It would be really awesome if you just stayed here and did that for the next several hours."

"So *now* am I forgiven?"

"We'll see. Shh." Rachel pulled him back to her, and before he could respond, she was sucking his bottom lip into her mouth and he moaned against her. Though the kissing intensified and Rachel knew for a fact she bore visible evidence of the make-out session on her neck, she was somewhat surprised when Bobby seemed content to not breach the barrier of her clothing. But it made her feel good at the same time. It was her own libido she had to restrain instead of fighting off his. It was a nice change of pace. She relaxed into the moment and loved every second of it.

She still wasn't sure what this meant about her sexual identity, but at the moment, she also didn't care. Fuck labels.

❖

Once Bobby left to go to work, Rachel retrieved her cell phone from the floor where it had fallen while they were kissing and saw that she had missed a few messages from Lori, which she ignored, and one call from Rory.

"Hey, the prodigal lesbian returns my call!"

"What did you just call me?"

"Which word is tripping you up, prodigal or lesbian?" Rory quipped.

"Allow me to respond to your not so clever jibe with an eighties retort. That was so funny, I forgot to laugh."

"Whatever, Shorty, I'm hilarious. You know it."

Rachel retorted with a line from a Bette Midler classic.

Rory groaned and said, "Great, now I have to resist the urge to start singing. Thanks for that earworm."

"You're welcome! So, anyway, why'd you call?"

"Yeah, I just wanted to check in and see how things were going with BobbyGate."

"There you go being clever again. How Maggie can stand living with you and not just laugh herself silly all day long, I'll never know."

"Amazingly, she somehow manages."

"Shocking."

"I know, right? So tell me," Rory said, serious for the first time since she answered the phone.

"What can I say? So far, I've managed to keep my clothes on."

"Wow, you must really like him."

Rachel sighed. "Yeah. But, more importantly, he really likes *me*. He's actually a nice guy and it's not about how great of a kisser he is, though he is *really* skilled in that area."

"It was never about that."

"No, no it wasn't. Rory, he's just super nice and kind of shy and he accepts all my craziness. And still comes back for more."

"Good. You deserve someone nice."

"I mean, don't get me wrong, I still have my hang-ups, those aren't gone, but I want to explore this."

"Maybe you'll find out something about yourself that you never knew before."

"What, that I like guys? I don't think that's going to happen. I think he's just an exception to the rule."

"Anything's possible, but that's not exactly what I meant."

"Okay, so what did you mean?" Rachel asked, confused.

"I just meant that you are able to look beyond the surface and see a person for who they really are and if they are worth knowing."

"Holy shit, that was freaky."

"What?"

"Finally, after years of trying and failing, I'm dating you. Holy shit!"

"What the hell are you talking about?"

"Well, Bobby said something really similar earlier about seeing people for who they really are. It just weirded me out hearing you say basically the same thing. I mean, I know you're not exactly alike, but I had no idea you guys were alike at all." Rachel was smiling, happy at the revelation.

"Oh my God, does he have curly red hair too?"

"Fuck you, Merida, that's not even funny. Ginger women are gorgeous, ginger men not so much. Don't even joke about that."

Rory was laughing. "I think you're being a little too hard on the Ron Weasleys of the world, don't you?"

"No, I do not. Okay, I should let you go for now. I'm sorry if I interrupted dinner prep or something."

"You did not. I'm not cooking tonight. Maggie is teaching until ten, so it's leftover night. I was just sitting here reading."

"Got it. I'm sorry that I never ask you about your classes or your relationship. I've been selfish lately."

"No, you haven't. You've just had more going on than me. My life is busy but pretty settled. I'm enjoying my classes and my relationship is awesome. There, all caught up."

"God, you guys just ooze cuteness. Have you even had an argument yet?"

"Yeah, actually, our first argument was before we left Illinois. We came really close to breaking up, all over a stupid misunderstanding. Since then we really don't fight. We talk to each other if we feel like something is bothering us. We don't let things fester. That being said, we still get annoyed with each other sometimes. But when we do, we try to quickly realize that by the time we get annoyed with each other it's because other things from outside stressors have just piled up, and me leaving my dirty dishes on the coffee table since breakfast is just the last thing Maggie needed to see that day. We give each other the space to be annoyed because we know that's going to happen. We're not the perfect couple—we just know how to handle our shit."

"Wow, you sound like a mature adult or something."

"Fuck you."

"And it's gone." Rachel chuckled.

"Whatever. But in all seriousness, I hope this works out for you."

"Thank you. Hey, Rory?"

"Yeah?"

"I really am happy for you too. I'm glad you have Maggie."

"I know you are."

Rachel smiled. "Talk to you later."

CHAPTER FIVE

Once she hung up the phone, Rachel decided she should follow Rory's example and do some of her own reading for class. Just as she was getting into her drama crit class text, there was a determined knock on her door. She sighed loudly and closed the book, then set it down on the bed before she stood up to answer. She tried not to sigh again when she saw that it was Lori. Rachel stood in the opening, blocking entrance into her room, keeping hold of the door.

"What do you want?"

"Wow, that was kind of rude, don't you think?" Lori sounded taken aback.

"Sorry, I'm busy. What do you want?" she repeated, not sorry at all.

"Okay, you're mad, I get that."

"I'm not mad. I just have stuff to do," Rachel said.

"Right. Anyway, I just wanted to talk to you about our fight the other day. I'm sorry."

"When did we fight?"

"Over the weekend, when you said I don't know you at all and I said some things and you stormed out. You haven't talked to me since, so I figured you were mad at me." Lori looked apologetic but Rachel had no tolerance for it anymore.

"Oh, you mean when you got all judgmental about who I choose to spend my time with. Now I remember."

"I wouldn't say judgmental. I was just really confused, that's all."

"As I recall, you were basically accusing me of either being bi or not knowing myself and I was saying you're wrong on both counts. Sounds kind of judgmental to me, to be honest. But that's just me." Rachel voice was starting to rise in anger and she tried to calm down.

"Can you blame me? I mean, what kind of lesbian dates dudes, even ones that used to be girls? Sounds kind of bi to me. But that's just me, I guess."

Calmness worked for all of five seconds. "Oh, cute, I see what you did there. You know, I wasn't mad five minutes ago, but I'm kind of working up to it. Go find a hobby. One that doesn't involve putting your nose into my business."

Rachel slammed her door, and then once it closed, flipped the bird in the general direction of where Lori would have been. She collapsed on the bed, grabbed a pillow from under her head, and screamed into it, half wishing she had screamed in Lori's face. When she was done, she smiled at the thought at how it would have echoed down the cinder block hallway, probably causing everyone on the floor to pop their heads out of their rooms like prairie dogs just to see what all the commotion was about.

Rachel put the pillow back under her head and pulled her phone out of her pocket. She texted Rory, *I really need to start keeping better company.*

Told you. Just keep your friends list down to the few who actually have your best interest in mind.

So far, that's only two people.

I assume you mean me and Bobby. At least we're the best people. Don't forget, Maggie and my parents are also Team Rachel.

Rachel felt her cheeks grow warm and a genuine smile played across her lips at the thought that she really was loved by the same people she herself loved and admired. Forgoing her usual humor, Rachel texted back, *I could use some cheerleaders right about now. Thank you.*

I'm always cheering for you.

❖

The one aspect of her stage combat class Rachel didn't care much for were the days they had lecture. Wednesday was just such a day. They were back in the classroom discussing the fight scenes from *Romeo and Juliet.* The discussion was enhanced by pages in their textbook, as well as Dr. Silver showing video clips from various movie versions and stage productions to show how the scenes were interpreted by various directors. Rachel was surprised there were lectures in a combat class; she'd expected it would be all fighting all the time. She had commented on that during the second week of class when they were told that the next class would meet in the classroom so they could go over some basics from the text.

"Yeah, I'm just confused as to why we are spending valuable class time on lectures, when there's so much fighting we could do."

"Well, if you had read the syllabus, this wouldn't come as a surprise. If the way I have structured this class is not to your liking, you still have time to drop it and take the movement class with Dr. Baskin next semester."

Rachel felt her face turning red as some of her classmates were looking in her direction. She felt she was being challenged, but she wasn't going to sink into her seat, all apologetic. "No, I just meant that I thought stage combat would be more hands-on, instead of reading and writing papers." According to the syllabus—that she had *definitely* read—there were three short papers that were due at various times during the semester and a presentation that was due at the end of the semester. Nothing too difficult by any means, but still not what she had expected.

"Ah, I see what you're saying there. Let me ask you this—do you think Harry Potter could have just summoned a Patronus if he hadn't been taught first?"

Polite snickers from the other students.

Rachel tried to fight back a grin. "Well, considering he was such a powerful wizard, I think he could have."

"Powerful wizard or not, he still had to be taught how to use and control that power. Without such instruction, he and those around him could have been hurt." Dr. Silver cocked her head to the side in a gesture Rachel was coming to recognize.

Rachel was happy to cross swords on the subject of Harry Potter against the worthiest of foes, even if that foe was her professor. "True. But all throughout the books, people got hurt regardless. It didn't seem to matter how much he knew. In fact, it seemed like the more he knew, the harder the challenges he had to face became."

"Such is life, is it not?"

"Granted, but maybe if there had been more doing and less reading he and his classmates wouldn't have screwed up as much as they did."

Some of her classmates seemed amused at the turn of events. Others had long since taken the opportunity to play on their phones or other electronic devices. But Rachel realized she was enjoying herself. She'd never realized how much fun it could be to spar with a teacher, even if the only weapon she was using was words.

Dr. Silver bowed her head slightly to Rachel, as if she was admitting defeat. "Perhaps, as the semester goes on, we will see which method works best. I will leave you with one thought before we get back to the lecture you are so impatient with—a hasty man drinks his tea with a fork. Think about that as I continue my lecture." With a bow and a playful smile, Dr. Silver had resumed her lecture.

Now, two weeks later, they were having their third classroom session of the semester. This one was done much the same way, with video clips interspersed with Dr. Silver lecturing. Rachel had learned her lesson after that first week. If she stopped being a smartass and actually paid attention, Dr. Silver definitely had something to teach her and the lectures were interesting. Plus, she had to admit, she was learning about technique.

Dr. Silver's biggest lesson, no matter that it had been presented in the geekiest way possible, had sunk in: *Good things come to those who wait.* She smiled to herself, thinking of the two bright red bruises on her neck. Surely there would be more good things in her future if she was only patient.

When class was over, Dr. Silver called out, "Rachel, can you come here a sec?"

Not sure what she was being singled out for, Rachel packed her books and gear into the beat-up old leather satchel she had found in a thrift store. It was light brown and scratched up and definitely had character. She threw it over her left shoulder as she walked up to the desk, confused. "What's up, Dr. S?"

Dr. Silver cocked an eyebrow at her but didn't correct her. "I was just going to ask if everything was okay."

"Yeah, everything's fine, why wouldn't it be?" Rachel shrugged.

"Well, you seemed distracted today, more so than usual, and I was wondering about that. Though I think I have an idea, now that I see you up close." Dr. Silver grinned and pointed, indicating Rachel's neck.

Embarrassed, Rachel immediately covered the side of her neck with her hand. She was sure her face was flaming. "I don't know what you're talking about."

"Uh-huh. It's not my job to bust your chops about having a social life. I just noticed you weren't paying much attention to my magnificent lecture and I know that's not like you. Normally, you never let an opportunity to challenge me go by. I've actually come to expect it. So is it just your social life that has your distracted, or is it something else?"

"So you like it when I fight back?"

"Well, I didn't at first. But I've come to see it differently. You're not fighting me but, rather, forcing me to up my game. And don't think I didn't notice what you did there. If you don't want to talk about anything, I can't make you, nor would I want to. Just wanted to let you know that if something was on your mind and you wanted to talk about it, you could." Dr. Silver tilted her head to the left and shrugged, giving Rachel a small smile.

"Okay. There is stuff going on, but I'm sure that's true with everybody. I'm sure even you have something going on that distracts you from time to time."

"As you say, don't we all? My point stands. I'm here if you need me."

"Thank you. I'll remember that. I gotta go. See you next week. I promise I'll be back to my old self and challenging whatever you're doing. Just because I can."

"Not just because you can. Just because it's fun."

"As you say." Rachel steepled her hands in front of her chest and gave a small bow. "Good day, Dr. S."

Dr. Silver chuckled. "Good day, Rachel."

Rachel waved as she walked out the door. She hadn't realized that she had been that distracted during class, to the point that it had been noticed. She had alternately been thinking about Bobby and Lori—more to the point, Lori's comments about how dating Bobby made Rachel look.

She was self-aware enough to know that she reacted so strongly to Lori because Lori was just voicing things that had been going through her mind since the night she'd met Bobby. Despite how much she liked him and wanted to explore whatever it was that was happening with him, she still wasn't sure.

But if she was honest, when they had been kissing on her bed the day before, the thought of him being trans hadn't crossed her mind at all. Instead, all she'd thought about was how great a kisser he was and wondering how long she could restrain herself from ripping off his clothes.

That thought was wonderful, but it also brought questions to mind about the general logistics of things. Would he wear a strap-on? Would he want to be touched? Would the binding he wore to flatten his chest come off?

And the question at the core of everything that bothered her the most: Would she still find Bobby attractive once his body started to change?

What did it mean about her sexuality if she was attracted to him and so willing to date a guy? Being bi was cool. The intellectual part of her brain would sometimes kick in and suggest that maybe she was bi…but she knew she really wasn't. She felt it in the core of her being that she was a lesbian. She had never been attracted to men. So why did the thought that people like Lori would think she was bi bother her so much?

She knew she should have been able to shake it off but she couldn't, and she couldn't explain why. Maybe she did need someone to talk to about these things, but would it feel weird talking to her professor? Of course, she had already discussed this with Rory. But she wanted a new perspective.

Did she have the courage to make Dr. Silver her confidant? How weird would that be? Maybe another day. Rachel sighed. One more thing she had an issue about apparently.

The following day, Rachel realized that she still wasn't sure what direction to go. She decided that maybe talking to Dr. Silver wasn't such a bad idea after all. What could it hurt? She knocked on Dr. Silver's office door somewhat tentatively. This was the first time she had ever had a reason to attend her office hours.

From within, Rachel heard Dr. Silver's soft voice say, "Come in."

Dr. Silver smiled at her as she walked in. "Ms. Cole. How can I help you?"

Rachel closed the door behind her and took a seat next to the desk.

"Well, you mentioned that I could come see you." Rachel wasn't sure why she felt so nervous. She wasn't sure if the professor actually was intimidating or if it was just the thought of talking to someone she hardly knew about something so personal.

Dr. Silver set her pen down, leaned back in her chair, and clasped her hands together. "Yes, yes, I did. What's on your mind?"

"Uh, well, it's kind of complicated."

"Naturally. Is it a school-related issue, or something more personal?"

The look Dr. Silver gave Rachel was intense but kind. All the same, it had the opposite effect than Rachel was sure the professor intended. Instead of putting her at her ease, when Rachel looked Dr. Silver in the eye, suddenly the kindness was too much. She stood up hastily.

"You know what, never mind. You're my professor, not my therapist, and this is a personal problem and not a school problem, so I should go. Sorry for bothering you." Rachel took a step toward the door.

"Rachel, wait." Dr. Silver's voice was commanding without being forceful. Rachel responded to it by turning around. "Do you drink coffee?"

"I'm sorry, what now?"

"Well, I was thinking it might be a good idea to get out of here and go someplace less stuffy."

Rachel considered. "Yeah, I drink coffee. Fine, I suppose I can let you buy me a cup of coffee."

Dr. Silver grinned. "Mind if we go Dutch?"

Rachel grinned back. "I get it. This is not a date."

Dr. Silver shook her head, her grin never wavering. "Something like that. Come on, let's go." Dr. Silver moved past her and opened the door, then gestured for Rachel to walk out ahead of her. Rachel walked out of the office, and Dr. Silver followed, locking her door behind her.

❖

They got coffee at the campus food court, then took the short walk to the man-made pond, found a bench with no one else around, and sat there in silence for a minute or two while Rachel sipped her coffee, the cup clasped with both hands, and Dr. Silver sat casually looking out at the water. Rachel had the feeling Dr. Silver was waiting for her to speak first, since the professor just sat there in companionable silence with a peaceful look on her face.

Finally, Rachel said, "I wonder how many people have fallen in love in front of this sad little hole in the ground. My best friend Rory had a nice romantic moment here. I did too, actually. Maybe there's magic here." Startled by her own thought, Rachel sipped from her cup again. *What's wrong with me? I am not a sentimental fool.*

Dr. Silver smiled. "That would be nice."

"Yeah. Bobby and I had our first kiss here."

"Really? Good spot for it."

"Yep. It was on the other side, over there." Rachel pointed to a spot on the other side of the pond. Dr. Silver nodded.

"Sounds like the start of something good."

"Something is the operative word. I'm not sure what to call it."

"Who says you have to define it at all?"

"That's true. I don't, I guess. Maybe if I stopped trying to do that, I wouldn't be having the problem I'm having right now."

"Which is?"

Rachel sighed. "Okay, first, if you don't know, I'm a lesbian."

"Okay. Me too."

"Really? Awesome! Sisterhood is powerful, amirite?" Rachel put up her fist and Dr. Silver bumped it, laughing.

"Right."

"So, I've been out since high school and I've had my share of relationships. Probably more than my share, if truth be known."

"Don't worry about that, that number means nothing in the grand scheme of things. Your body and your heart are to do with as you wish," Dr. Silver said vehemently. "Sorry, getting off my soapbox now. Go on."

"Thank you for saying that. You're right. Anyway, I've got a type I'm generally attracted to—butches, you know? The kind that wear men's clothes and have short haircuts, and fix things and have dirt under their nails and play sports. The point is, I have a type I generally gravitate toward, and when I met Bobby, I thought Bobby fit into that category fine but there was a little problem."

"Not as butch as you thought?"

"Um, no, not that. Bobby's a...Bobby's trans."

"Ah, I see. That is an interesting predicament."

"Yeah. I mean, I'm not bi, never have been. I'm pretty secure in that. But other people are going to think I am. Some of my friends have already accused me of it—well, accused is the wrong word. Labeled, I guess. I just don't know if I want to spend the rest of my life explaining that."

"Sounds like you need new friends, friends who wouldn't need an explanation."

"Beginning to think the same thing."

"Rachel, can I ask you a question?" Dr. Silver turned so that she was facing Rachel, and Rachel did the same, with one knee resting on the bench.

"Anything you want."

"Did you know I was gay before I mentioned it?"

"No, actually it never occurred to me. Unlike my best friend, I try not to think about my professors' sex lives."

Dr. Silver laughed. Sobering, she said, "The reason I asked is to make this point. You wouldn't have known I was gay if I hadn't chosen to out myself to you. Because I present myself the way I do, my sexuality is not readily apparent, unlike the butches you are attracted to, whose sexuality is apparent in their clothing and their walk, as well as other external factors. I am what one of my friends calls stealth gay. I accept this about myself and in accepting it, I also know that I will spend the rest of my life choosing whether or not to come out to people, based on the circumstances. But it's my choice as well as it is yours and just a fact of life I accept in order to live my life the way I want to."

"That makes sense and I get it, but it's more than that. It's other people's assumptions I don't think I can handle."

"People are always going to assume something about you that isn't true, based more on their preconceived notions than your actual behavior. That's not something you can control, so you shouldn't waste your time worrying about it. Personally, I think the main thing to think about is how you really feel about this young man and what kind of relationship you want to have with him. The rest will work itself out in time. And besides, I imagine, like me, sometimes you already have to out yourself. This shouldn't be much different."

Rachel nodded her head thoughtfully. "You make a lot of sense."

"Of course. They don't just give these jobs away, you know." They shared a smile, and then Dr. Silver gave Rachel a sideways glance. "Are you sure the thought of your own identity is the only thing that worries you?"

Rachel returned the sideways look. "Well…there are a couple other things."

"Such as?"

Rachel shrugged. "What if I'm not attracted to him when he starts to change? What if the sex is weird?" Then, much softer, she voiced her main concern. "What if I'm not strong enough for him?"

Dr. Silver exhaled. "Those are some weighty things to be concerned about."

"Yeah."

"First of all, he's not suddenly going to turn into a were-wolf. From my friends who've transitioned, I can say that the bodily changes that occur are gradual and may take years. I doubt you will even notice them all that much. As for the sex, all sex is weird, but sex is sex and, no matter how you come together or what genders you are, always has to be negotiated so both parties have mutual enjoyment. As for the last one, if this is a relationship built upon understanding and is meant to last, you will become his biggest ally whether you realize it or not. That is all the wisdom a cup of coffee gets you, I'm afraid. I just hope it was helpful."

Rachel slowly smiled. "Yeah, yeah, it was. What I took from that is you're telling me to get my shit together, it's not all about me, but if I care about him it'll all work out one way or another, and to just not think about it."

Dr. Silver laughed. "If that's what you got out of it and it's useful, then yes, that's what I said."

"Okay, I can do that. Thanks, Dr. S."

"Call me Lou. Though not in class, don't want the others to get jealous." Lou gave Rachel a sardonic smile.

"God forbid. Or think I'm doing what Rory did."

"Oh, yes. I've heard about that. So Rory's your friend?"

"Yeah. She may be hot for teacher, but I do not suffer from that malady. That is, of course, unless we're talking about Dr. Baskin. No offense."

Lou laughed. "None taken. I wish them much happiness and think what happened to them, that she felt she had to leave, was shitty. But, by the same token, I'm not into dating my students. Not that I'm judging her in the slightest, just not my thing."

"Good. I want to earn my A the old-fashioned way, by coasting most of the semester, then fevered panic during finals."

"And you shall. I play no favorites."

"Wouldn't want you to."

"Just glad I could help." Lou stood up from the bench. "Now I need to go. Pages to grade before I sleep, pages to grade before I sleep. I'll see you in class, Ms. Cole."

"Yes, you will."

As Dr. Silver walked away, Rachel stayed where she was, looking out at the calm water. She realized that she wanted her life to be like that pretty little man-made hole in the ground: calm but magical.

CHAPTER SIX

Bobby was sitting on his brother's couch, zoned out, playing some violent video game, when his brother Chris came in wearing nothing but flannel boxers and carrying a large bowl of cereal. He sat down next to Bobby and proceeded to eat his breakfast.

After a minute or two of Bobby not acknowledging his presence, Chris spoke. "Why are you playing this?"

"I don't even know what *this* is."

"How can you not know?"

"It's what was in the machine. I get to kill things. Violently. That's all I care about."

"I respect that." The silence grew between them for another minute or two. "Behind you."

"Yeah, I know. I can actually see that, you know?"

"Yeah, yeah."

A couple of bites later and Bobby was still staring at the screen, almost trancelike.

"All right, what's wrong?" Chris asked.

"Nothing. I'm doing well. Look at my score."

"You know what I mean. Why are you killing things in the first place? I thought you hated stuff like this."

Bobby shrugged. "Felt like it."

Chris set his now empty bowl on the coffee table, and then sat back into the corner of the couch. "Little bro, I've known you how long?"

Bobby didn't answer, but a corner of his mouth lifted in a smile.

"I know something ain't right with you. Are you going to tell me or am I going to have to beat it out of you?" Chris knuckle punched Bobby on the shoulder, not very lightly.

"Ow, you fucker!" Bobby paused his game and smacked his brother on the bare thigh, causing Chris to yelp and making Bobby laugh. "That's what you get."

"Fine, don't talk to me, asshole, see if I care."

"Why are you so interested in my sex life, anyway?"

"Who said anything about your sex life? What's wrong with your sex life? I thought you were seeing some hot blond chick?"

Bobby leaned back against the couch with a sigh. "So did I. She hasn't called or texted me in three days."

"So? I thought things like that didn't bother you."

"I'm usually good with it because I know everyone's busy. But this is different. I know she's had issues about dating a trans guy. It just makes me worry that she's changed her mind or something." He shrugged. "I don't know, I guess I thought she was different and would be able to get over it. Guess I was wrong."

"Wow, that sucks. Well, there's other chicks in the sea. You've never had a problem getting laid. Don't let this one get to you."

"But I *want* this one. And I thought she wanted me."

"You know, Little Man, that communication works both ways, right?"

"You think I haven't texted her? I've sent her a couple of texts and she hasn't responded. I don't want to send more than that and look pathetic. I just miss her. I thought we really connected." Bobby shifted his gaze to the side dejectedly.

"Dude, if you're going to be a guy, you gotta grow some balls."

Bobby laughed. "It doesn't quite work that way."

"No, I mean, grow a pair!"

"I wish I could!"

"No, I meant…be bold, don't just sit around here and mope. Don't be a pussy just because you still have one." Chris caught Bobby's wrist before he could land the blow.

"Asshole. Let go." Bobby struggled to pull his arm free. Chris released him and he rubbed his wrist.

"I meant, chase her. Show up at her door. Don't just sit here being a punk-ass bitch," Chris said goading him.

"Maybe. We'll see."

"If you don't, you'll turn into one of those folks who sit on the couch all day playing video games and arguing with twelve-year-olds. If you don't make a move, someone else will. Go find a way to be a hero in real life and get off my couch."

"I never knew you were such a romantic," Bobby teased.

"Fuck you. Now I have to go get dressed and pick up Marissa. See you later. Remember what I said." Chris got off the couch, picked up his bowl, and left the room.

"Be a hero." Bobby's voice trailed off, as he stayed where he was, lost in thought.

"Okay, so why haven't you talked to him in three days?" Rory sounded confused, as well as slightly annoyed, although Rachel wasn't sure why Rory would be pissed at her.

"Can't a girl have second thoughts?" Rachel lay back on her bed, one knee up with her other foot crossed on top of it. She started to twirl her hair, a nervous habit she hated. She stopped abruptly.

"Yeah, but I think you're on your third or fourth thoughts. What's the deal?"

"I just want to be sure. I don't want to lead him on."

Rory sighed. "Stop it." This time there was no question she was annoyed.

"Stop what?"

"Stop letting the rest of the world get to you. I thought you had put that issue to rest. You told off Lori, you made out with him, and you got a sizable hickey for good measure. So what the hell happened that made you third-guess yourself?"

Rachel sighed. "Nothing special. Just thinking too much."

"Well, stop that too. All thinking does is get you in trouble. Who was it who scolded me when I said I had to have a think about proposing to Maggie? Who was it who said I should propose because I love her? That I didn't need a better reason?"

"Well, of course that great advice came from me, but what does that have to do with me and Bobby? I sure as hell am not ready to propose to the boy." Rachel giggled.

"Fine, let me amend it to something more befitting your situation. *Because you like him.* Do you need a better reason to talk to him and go out with him? Seriously, do you think I would be where I am today with the woman I love if I had stopped and overthought the whole damn thing? I just went for it. I chased her, romanced her, backed off when she wasn't sure, but then I was back on her doorstep when she was really ready. Oh, man, I never told you this, but when I got that text that night asking me to come back, I was almost back to the dorm. I ran all the way back to her house. I didn't want her to change her mind. I didn't think about it, I just did it."

"Aww. Well, I did not call you the queen of the big romantic gesture for nothing. But why isn't he running to my door, all out of breath?"

"Maybe he doesn't know you want him. You haven't talked to him in three days. Maybe he thinks you don't want to see him again. Maybe you should do something really drastic and, oh, I don't know, call or text him. Just a thought."

"Yeah, I know. Maybe you're right." Rachel sighed in defeat.

"Of course I'm right."

"How can that be? I'm the one who's always supposed to be right in this relationship." Just as they were sharing a laugh, there was a knock on the door. "Hold on," Rachel said, "there's someone here. I'm taking you with to the door."

"Wonderful."

Rachel extricated herself from the bed and opened the door, half expecting Lori to be standing there and preparing herself for round two. She was totally surprised to find Bobby standing there with his usual cocky grin. He gave her a little wave.

"Holy shit," Rachel said.

"Is it him?" Rory asked.

"Yeah, it's him." Somewhat confused at seeing him there, Rachel stared at him and asked, "What are you doing here?"

"Don't ask him that, you moron!" Rory's voice interjected. "Just ask him in. I'm going to hang up now. Good luck and don't screw this up."

Rachel took the phone from her ear and said to Bobby, "I'm sorry, that was rude. Come on in."

"Thank you."

Once the door was closed, Rachel said, "Sorry I haven't texted you back. I really don't even have a good reason, I was just thinking...a lot."

"Well, no good can come from that."

"Yeah, so I've heard. Look, I'm sorry for being so flaky. You deserve better than that. I really do like you, I do, I just, I don't know if—"

Bobby cut her off in a crushing hug and kiss. It would have been the most romantic thing ever, if he hadn't stepped on her foot in the rush to take her into his arms. They broke apart to Rachel's giggles and Bobby's embarrassment.

"Oh, geez, I'm sorry. Are you okay?" Bobby was turning red and he wasn't smiling or laughing about it. He looked mortified.

Rachel stopped giggling and cupped his face in her hands and smiled at him. "Yeah, I'm fine. Why don't we try it slower, hmm? Maybe more like this?" Rachel put both arms around his neck and reached up to him for a kiss. He gave her a small smile and obliged, then drew her to him, wrapping his arms around her waist.

"Yeah, slower is much better," he said.

"Can we start over?"

"You can do that as many times as you like."

Rachel giggled. "Oh, I will, but I meant you and me. Maybe really start this time? Maybe even go on a real date."

"A real date? Like out in public and everything?"

"Yeah, stud, a real date. But not just yet. I kind of like having you all to myself right now."

"Oh, you do, do you? And why is that?"

"Let's just say you're going to be busy. Or not. I might just torture you, then send you home."

"Oh, that would be so cruel."

"Not cruel. Delicious agony."

Bobby groaned and lunged for her neck and began to work on the fading mark. Rachel laughed as she clung to him, enjoying the slight pain as he sucked on the hollow between her neck and her shoulder. At times it hurt, but at others, it felt so good. She moaned and clutched his hair in her hand. After several moments, she couldn't stand it any longer and she pulled hard on his hair and brought him up for a hungry kiss.

Bobby let her set the pace. Though Rachel was as turned on as she had ever been, she wasn't ready to go beyond kissing. She was normally not shy about sharing her body with someone but this time was different for her, and she couldn't say why.

❖

For their first official date, Rachel and Bobby chose to have a picnic at the pond, because, as Rachel said, she really just wanted to be with him somewhere without a lot of distractions, where she could just enjoy his company.

"You mean it has nothing to do with not wanting to be seen with me in public?" Bobby asked, with the hint of a smile, though Rachel saw through it.

"Bobby Layton, I will not tolerate any self-pity or whatever you want to call it. Has it not occurred to you that maybe I just want you all to myself? So I can make you blush. So I can make you squirm." As she said it, she trailed her fingers up his arm and he shivered. She laughed evilly. "Yeah, like that."

Bobby narrowed his eyes at her and said, "Careful, I have no problem making a scene."

"You mean like making out in public?"

"Yeah. Or pushing you into the water." He laughed and his chocolate eyes danced.

"You wouldn't dare!"

"Try me."

After staring him down, Rachel said, "Maybe later you can get me wet."

Bobby narrowed his eyes at her, but instead of picking up the sexual gambit she threw, he said teasingly, "Chicken."

"I'm definitely not chicken." With that declaration, she grabbed him by his shirt and pulled him to her for a kiss. What started as quick and forceful became sensual and languorous, until she moaned and had to push him away. "Damn, you're good at that."

"I'm glad you think so."

"I'm sure I'm not the only one."

"Ah, are we about to get into our respective dating histories? If so, I'm okay with that. What do you want to know?" As he talked, Bobby put the remains of their lunch back into the cooler he had packed their food in.

Rachel stretched out, resting on her elbows, and crossed her feet at the ankles. "I don't need to know about all that crap, as long as you were safe. I'm the last person to get hung up on ex-girlfriends."

"Or ex-boyfriends?"

Rachel eyed him for a moment then shrugged. "Eh, past is past. Were you safe?"

Bobby stretched out next to her, turned on his side, and rested his head on his hand. "Every time, Rachel, every time."

She mimicked his posture. "Well, I've never slept with guys, but let's just say, when it was necessary, I was safe. This is boring, I don't want to talk about this stuff."

"Okay, what do you want to talk about?"

"Tell me more about you. Tell me about your music. You want to be famous?"

Bobby laughed. "I just want people to hear my songs and like them. I don't need fame and fortune, just an appreciative audience."

"So you would be happy delivering pizzas for the rest of your life, as long as you got to sing in front of a crowd?"

"Well, maybe not pizzas, but in a way, yeah. I mean, for me, it's not about making tons of money and living like a king. I don't want to be chewed up and spit out by an industry that's going to make me do music I don't like, simply to make them money. I want to do what I want to do, even if it means I won't be able to buy shiny things." Bobby smiled and shrugged.

"I get it, you have integrity. I respect that. And just so you know, I'm not the kind of girl who likes expensive shiny things, so don't worry about that. That is, if you were."

"I wasn't. I could tell that about you, Rachel."

"Really, how?"

"You just don't seem to be into material things all that much. Plus, I've had girls turn me down when they find out what my job is. They think a singer is romantic but a pizza boy is white trash or something and they don't want to be seen with me."

"Some girls only want boys who buy them the shiny. They make the rest of us look bad. I only want you to be real with me and treat me like a person."

"I can do that." Bobby leaned in and placed a small kiss on her lips.

When he pulled away, Rachel smiled. "I really like you, even when you're being a dork."

He laughed. "I really like you too." He paused then asked, "So, what else do you want to know about me?"

"You told me on the first day that you changed your name to distance yourself from your family. Do you not speak to them at all?"

"Well, I live with my brother and he's okay with things. Said he always wanted a brother. My parents—well, they're assholes." Bobby shifted his gaze and inclined his head.

Rachel gently nudged his chin so he was looking her in the eye again. "You can tell me. This is the part I want to know. Take your time—I'm not in a hurry."

Bobby put his hand on her waist and said, "Not much to tell. I came out as bi in high school and they ignored it, didn't take it seriously. Then, when I came out as trans four years ago, that's when they said they only have one son and one daughter and it didn't matter what I called myself, I would always be a girl. And if I kept up this nonsense, then I was out of the family. So I guess I'm out of the family. At least as far as they're concerned. They don't know I'm living with Chris. If they did, they'd probably disown him too."

"Fuck those assholes. They may be your parents but they aren't your family and they don't get to have a say into who you are. Your family is what you make it." Rachel caressed his cheek.

"Yeah, you're right. The hell with them." Then he kissed her. They lay there kissing for quite some time, until Bobby realized what time it was and that he had to go to work, but not before walking her to her door and giving her a nice leisurely kiss in her hallway.

She stepped back and pushed him away. "Go away now, go on. Go deliver pizzas. Make some dough."

He rolled his eyes. "I'll see you." He waved then walked to the elevator.

Just as Rachel was unlocking her door, Molly came out of the bathroom. "Hey, Rachel." She smiled.

Rachel had always liked Molly. She just thought the girl clung too much to whatever Lori said, instead of doing her own thing and thinking her own thoughts. She returned her smile. "Hey, Molly."

"Hey, Rach?"

"Yeah?"

"Thanks."

"For what?"

"What you said the other day about it being okay to be attracted to someone, no matter what. Okay, that's not exactly what you said, but I'm just glad you said it. Sometimes Lori gets to be too much, you know what I mean?" Molly was practically whispering, which was understandable, considering how much sound carried in their hallway.

"I know what you mean and that's putting it mildly."

"Right. I mean, if truth be known, I'm not a lesbian, I'm bi, but she hates it when I even mention it. I don't know what her problem is."

"Me neither, but I think you and I need a better class of friends. I gotta go, but hit me up if you want to hang out without whatshername."

"I will. Oh, and Rach?"

"Yeah?"

"He really does have awesome eyes."

"God, I know, right?" Rachel nodded to her now open door. "You want to come in and gush?"

Laughing, Molly said, "Sure."

"Good. I can tell you all about the sweet boy with the sexiest eyes you've ever seen."

CHAPTER SEVEN

A few nights later, Rachel sent Bobby a text that left no room for argument. *You are taking me out for a hamburger. You get no say in the matter. Pick me up, ASAP.*

Bobby and Rachel were sitting across from each other at the old fifties-themed diner on the east side of town that only a small scattering of students ever went to. Most of the clientele were what Rachel thought of as old-timers, who more than likely had been going to the diner since it opened. She was more than okay with there not being a lot of students there, because when it came to how she wanted to spend her time, she was increasingly moving more toward Rory's way of thinking: the less people around at one time the better. She wished Rory were here now to share in her new relationship but she couldn't be and there was no point in dwelling on that fact. Instead, she wanted to enjoy the moment with Bobby and spend as much time with him as their schedules allowed.

She sat across from him now with a plate full of the best burger and fries she'd ever tasted, along with an old-fashioned root beer float. She pulled the cherry off her drink when she knew she had his attention and slowly sucked the cherry off the stem, keeping her eyes locked with his.

He grinned and chuckled somewhat uncomfortably. "You always this mean to your dates?"

She threw back her head and laughed evilly. "You think this is mean, wait until you see what I can do with this cherry stem." She held the stem up for emphasis but before she could put it in her mouth to demonstrate her point, he snatched it out of her hand and put it on his side of the table out of her reach. She laughed again. "Now who's chicken?"

Bobby leaned in and lowered his voice. "I'm not chicken either, but unless you want me to leap across this table and make a scene that would more than likely get us thrown out, you'll stop torturing me." Then he gave her a small kiss on the lips and Rachel smiled at him before he sat back.

Rachel got an evil glint in her eye. "I double dog dare ya."

"Why do I get the feeling that it's always going to be an adventure with you?"

"Would that be so bad?"

"Nah. But I don't know how often I'm going to have enough cash on me for bail money." He grinned and she laughed at him.

"Take it as it comes, my boy, take it as it comes."

Bobby sighed. "I'm really glad you keep calling me but I have to ask you something."

"What's that?"

"Do you ever let yourself get serious? I mean, every time we get on the verge of a serious conversation, you back away from it. I'm not criticizing you—I was just curious." He reached for her hand across the table and squeezed it. She squeezed back and gave him a small smile in return.

"So you've noticed that, have you?"

"Yeah, I have. I haven't said anything because I really don't like to make an issue of things, but I just hope that you feel comfortable enough with me to talk about important stuff. You're really good at turning the conversation back to me. Is it because there are just some things you don't feel comfortable talking about or don't know how?"

"Oh, my sweet boy…you really are sweet. And no, I wasn't turning it around to you that time, just speaking the truth." She sighed. "I've just never been good at self-disclosure. We don't do much of it in my family. Hell, we don't talk much at all in my family. Rory can get me to talk sometimes, but not always. I guess I feel that everyone has their own problems, and they don't want to hear mine, so why don't I just suck it up and deal with my shit and try to help people deal with what they can't deal with. But if you ask me direct questions, I'll do my best to answer them, how's that?" She looked away, grabbed a fry, then looked back at him questioningly. He was still holding her hand.

"Okay, I guess I do have a question." He knew how harshly the words themselves might be taken, so he was careful to keep any accusation from his voice. "Why did you call me that first time if you're such a die-hard lesbian?"

Rachel looked startled at the question. "Oh, that."

"Yeah, that."

"Well, I did have to think about it some and talk to Rory about it some but"—she shrugged—"I just like you. That's what I realized. And I don't care what anyone else has to say about that. I'm me, I know who that is, and anyone who thinks they know me but really doesn't, who makes assumptions about me, can just piss off. It's about me, not about them."

Bobby grinned. "That sounds like a song."

"Well, then write it."

"Maybe I will." After a moment, he said, "I have another question."

She let go of his hand to pick up her drink with both hands, one hand on the straw. "Go ahead."

Bobby leaned back against the seat and asked, "Did you ever date Rory?"

Rachel choked on her drink. She coughed, set the drink back on the table, and grabbed a napkin to wipe her mouth. "Wow, what a question."

"As I said before, it's okay if you have feelings for her other than friendship. I just want to know."

She challenged him with her eyes. "Why would you want to know that?"

"Because I want to know if you will ever care about me as much as you care about her." There was no smile on his face. He was completely serious.

Rachel paused so she could choose her words carefully. When she spoke she spoke softly and looked him directly in the eyes. She wasn't afraid of this honesty. "I do love Rory with all my heart. I have from the moment we met in an acting class as undergrads. We hit it off spectacularly and I thought we were on the verge of dating, especially when she started kissing me after we wrapped *Rent*. But she backed off and let me down easy. I couldn't be mad about it. Knowing she's in love with Maggie hasn't diminished how I feel about her but I wholeheartedly want her to be happy and have love in her life—and she is, and she does. My feelings for her won't go away. I've accepted that, but I believe they will change in time. There is room in my heart to fall in love with someone else and I'm open to it. You shouldn't worry about that. That is, if you were." She put her hand palm up on the table and curled her fingers, asking him to take her hand, which he did.

"I'm glad. I didn't want to have to compete with a ghost."

"You're not competing with her or anyone. This is all about you." She leaned in and he met her halfway with a kiss.

When he pulled away there was a smile on his face. "You make me hear music, Rachel."

"Now that's a first. Most of my lovers don't hear music until they see me naked."

"They may see you with your clothes off but I don't think anyone has ever seen you as naked as you just were."

"I think you're right about that." Rachel looked at him, really looked, not paying any attention to the rest of the diners, who ceased to exist for her at that moment.

"Well, if it isn't the bisexual and the beast." Lori's voice from across the room shattered her focus. She was at their table a moment later with Lanie in tow, their arms crossed over their chests and sneers on their lips.

"Out enjoying themselves just like couples do. Isn't that cute?" Lori added acidly.

Bobby let go of Rachel's hand and sat back, narrowing his eyes at their intruders and clenching his jaw.

Rachel could tell he was trying to restrain his anger, possibly because he thought they were still friends of hers and he was trying to be polite or because he was just trying not to make a scene in public. Rachel wasn't sure, but she felt no compunction either way. Oh, there was going to be a fucking scene, all right, Rachel was sure of it.

She sat back in her seat and looked up at Lori. She spoke to Bobby but her eyes never left Lori's face. "Oh, look, honey, it's that bitch I was telling you about who thinks she knows what she's talking about but really doesn't."

Bobby said nothing, just swallowed and exhaled angrily. His eyes went from Rachel to Lori and back again.

"I'm a bitch because I tell the truth?"

"No, you're a bitch because you are mean and think your truth is reality." Rachel stood up to Lori, who backed up a step. Her words were spoken quietly but directly. "If you don't shut your mouth and leave us the fuck alone, I'm going to shut it for you. Want to try me?" Rachel leaned in closer, staying in Lori's space, making her threat clear.

Bobby stood up and took Rachel's arm. "Remember when I said I didn't have bail money?" he joked as he gently tugged on her arm.

Without breaking eye contact with Lori, Rachel said, "Don't worry, I'm not going to hit her. She's not worth it. Let's go." She let Bobby lead her out, the whole time giving dirty looks over her shoulder, not caring about the looks they were now getting from the other diners.

❖

"Who the fuck does she think she is? Thinking she can just come up and say shit like that?" They were in Rachel's car but she had given Bobby the keys, as she knew she was too angry to drive. She wanted to rant instead and was sure Bobby would be steadier on the road than she would be at the moment.

Bobby asked, "So do you really know how to fight?"

Rachel, thrown out of her anger for a moment by the question, laughed. "The closest I've come to knowing how to fight is from watching these kung fu videos in class. And the videos looked more like dance videos then something I could use for self-defense. But she doesn't know that." At that declaration, her anger was fueled again.

"Why is she so angry about who you date, anyway? Why is it any of her business?"

Rachel let out an exasperated sigh. "Full disclosure?"

"That would be nice."

She put her hand on his knee. Bobby didn't take either hand off the wheel, which she wished he would have, but she let it pass and kept her hand where it was. "We kinda, sorta dated. Okay, if I'm being totally honest, we didn't date, we just had sex a few times. She wanted to date but I never did. I just wanted to keep it casual, you know? She couldn't handle it and got kind of obsessive for a while but then backed off and we became friends for a while. She's just a major pain in my ass and I should have never slept with her in the first place but I did and I can't change that."

"You broke her heart."

"I didn't mean to!"

"I know that. Just as Rory didn't mean to break your heart by falling in love with…Maggie, right?"

"Yeah. And I never said Rory broke my heart."

"But didn't she?"

"What do you mean?"

"Think about it. You gave her your heart and she didn't want it. She only wanted Maggie. I know that had to hurt."

"It did, but why are you trying to get me to be mad at her?"

"I'm not, just trying to understand that girl from the diner, who, granted, should not treat people that way and I have no idea what she's done before now, but I don't know, I just think she deserves our compassion. I've always felt that if you can understand where your enemy is coming from, you might be able to defuse a bad situation. I don't always succeed, but I'm always trying to understand." He shrugged, then finally did take his hand off the steering wheel and laid it on hers. He clasped her hand with his, then lifted it to his lips and kissed it.

She sighed contentedly. "I firmly believe you could single-handedly bring about world peace if everyone just tried to do things your way."

He laughed, sounding surprised and embarrassed. "I don't know about that, but maybe I can take a stab at it with my music." Then he began to sing the refrain from "I'd Like to Teach the World to Sing," and Rachel joined him. They laughed together as they continued to sing.

When the song ended, Rachel said, "Wow, that was cheesy. I'm glad I can be cheesy with you."

"Yeah, me too."

"Bobby?"

"Yeah?"

"Stay with me tonight?"

He stole a glance at her and she smiled coyly.

He exhaled slowly. "Are you sure?"

"Yeah, I am. I'd say it's about time, wouldn't you?"

"Only if you're sure."

"I'm not a virgin, remember?"

"Neither am I."

"It's time, Sweet Boy, it's time."

"Yeah, it is." He gave her the sweetest smile and his eyes caught the light of the passing streetlights and they shined.

As they rode up to the tenth floor, they took advantage of the fact that they were alone in the elevator. They started their dance as Bobby put his arms around her waist and pulled her hungrily to him for a kiss. She pressed him against the railing and leaned into him, putting her hand on the back of his neck. She sucked on his bottom lip as his hands grabbed her ass and she moaned against him.

It was a quick ride up and when the car jolted to a stop on her floor, she pushed away from him, smiled up at the security camera in the corner of the elevator, and waved. "Hope that was as good for you as it was for me," she said to the anonymous eye of the lens. Then she grabbed Bobby's hand and pulled him behind her down the hallway toward her door.

She hurriedly unlocked her door and, once it was open, pulled him in behind her and he kicked the door closed with his foot. He stumbled into her and, chuckling, she put her hands on his chest to steady him. "It's okay, baby, don't worry about it." She grabbed him by the belt and walked backward toward the bed, pulling him along. She sat down on the edge of the bed, her hands still on his waist. He stood above her, stroking her hair.

"You're sure about this?"

She didn't say a word. She only smiled and locked eyes with him as she proceeded to undo his black leather belt very slowly. Once undone, she unbuttoned his pants and pulled down his zipper. "Can I touch you?"

The look Bobby gave her was one of such tenderness as well as desire. But when he spoke, his voice hesitated. "Yes."

Whispering, Rachel said, "It'll be all right. I'll be gentle." Instead of plunging in, Rachel first rubbed the crotch of his pants, pushing against the seam.

He put his head back and closed his eyes. Slowly, very slowly, she put her hand inside and pushed against his clit. She just cupped him at first, then very lightly rubbed her thumb over the tip in a slow, rhythmic motion. He pushed his pants down his hips and shimmied until they fell to his ankles, and he stood there in just his boxers while her hand was inside them. He grabbed onto the railing of the top bunk to steady himself while Rachel continued to explore. As her fingers played with the opening, he tightened his grip on the bed and moaned out loud.

Rachel chuckled. "You like that?"

"Yes." He stammered when he responded.

"Can I do more than this?"

"Please."

She grinned at the stutter his desire was giving him. Gently she pulled his boxers down as he stood in front of her splendidly naked from the waist down. She took a breath. The sight was beautiful. Somehow she knew that no matter how much his body changed she would always find him beautiful, even when his body squared off and hollowed out and became manlier. He was just beautifully made and she wanted to do this right. She put her hands on his hips to bring him closer to her and she put her lips to him and sucked in the tip of his clit, then quickly released it, causing him to exhale and push himself into her. She gripped him tighter and started to lick his labia, nibbling here and there, causing him to cry out in such a way that could only mean one thing and she was sure her neighbors heard and understood and she didn't give a damn. *Let him cry out his bliss,* she thought. He had a right to it and she was more than happy to give it to him.

As her licking intensified, so did the movement of his hips. He continued to sway and push himself into her mouth with his hands on the back of her head. Finally, after a second cry out, he pushed himself away from her and tilted her chin up and kissed her hungrily. When he pulled away, he said, "My turn."

"But I'm not done with you."

"You are for now. My turn, I said." He pushed her back on the bed, kicking himself free of his pants, and pulled his shirt off over his head. Underneath was an undershirt and the binder he'd mentioned to her before. It zipped up like a vest. He paid little heed to these garments as he took them off as well and threw them aside.

She smiled at him and went to pull her own clothes off, but he stopped her.

"Wait for it." He grinned, then pushed up her blouse and bra and slowly lifted them over her head. When her breasts were revealed to him, he sighed in contentment. "Oh, Rachel, you are beautiful." He reached out to her and lightly touched her breast.

"So are you. Now you better finish what you started."

"Always do." He followed up his words by taking her nipple into his mouth, and as his teeth clamped down she let out a surprised cry of pleasure. He took his time with her nipples, giving each of them his utmost attention and driving her out of her mind.

Finally, she couldn't stand the sweet torture anymore and grabbed him by the hair, pulled his face away, and said, "For the love of God, fuck me now. Please."

He grinned as he caressed his fingers down her belly and to her clit. He teased her there, just as she had teased him. She moaned in protest and it made him grin. She pushed on his arm to try to make him enter her and he understood her message perfectly.

As he entered her, he said, "I'm not going to fuck you, I'm going to make love to you." Then he brought her to orgasm with piston-like insistence and she cried out several times before she fell back, limp on her pillows, his hand at rest but still inside her.

Her body rippled with aftershocks and he kissed her forehead as she snuggled into him. He pulled his hand free and put it to rest on her hip. "You okay?"

Her voice was unsteady when she answered. "Yes. I'm more than okay."

He chuckled. "Good." He pulled the covers up to their waists and kissed her lightly on the lips. "It was definitely time."

"Oh yeah. If you don't mind, can't talk right now." She put her hand on his chest and closed her eyes.

CHAPTER EIGHT

Rachel called Rory as soon as Bobby left.

"To what do I owe the pleasure of this call on this fine Saturday morning?" Rory asked.

"Oh, the pleasure was all mine, let me tell you," Rachel gushed.

"Rachel Cole, if I didn't know any better, I'd say that you've just gotten lucky. Have you gotten lucky?" There was much amusement in Rory's voice and Rachel could just picture the grin on her face.

"Oh, I got very lucky, in more than one way. Oh my God, he's the sweetest person on the fucking planet."

Rory laughed. "So you're saying he's a sensitive lover?"

"A lady doesn't kiss and tell."

"That's why I asked *you*."

"Asshole."

Ignoring her, Rory asked, "So, you finally gave him the golden ticket, huh? What'd he do to deserve that?"

"Nothing. And everything. Oh my God, Rory...I've never gushed over anyone before and I can't keep the stupid grin off my face. I look just like you did when I caught you playing that old fart's music that one day."

"Excuse you? That old fart was Louis Armstrong and he deserves your respect."

"Yeah, yeah. Focus, Morgan, we're talking about important things here."

"I will not have you desecrate a great musician like that. Not on my watch, Rachel Cole. Not when he got me and Maggie together."

"Louis Armstrong got you together?" Rachel asked, doubtfully.

"Yeah. We had our first dance and kiss to Louis. I think it serves as a good beginning. Did the two of you have any special music?"

Rachel burst out laughing. "Only if you count that hippie song they turned into a Coke commercial."

"You made out to a song about world peace?"

Rachel snickered. "I guess you had to be there."

"I'm glad I wasn't."

Rachel could barely contain her hysterics when she said, "You were there in spirit."

"I don't think I want to know what that means."

Ignoring her, Rachel said, "Oh, but I didn't tell you what led up to it. I almost punched Lori."

"Rachel, I did not know you found violence such a turn on. This makes me see you in such a new way."

"Didn't I tell you to focus? This is a good story. Are you going to be a good girl and listen?" Rachel asked, amused.

Rory rattled off a bit of dialogue from *My Fair Lady* about Eliza's protestations about being a good girl.

Rachel sighed and shook her head. "Your British accent needs work."

"You know I suck at accents." Rory was quiet a moment, as if listening to someone else, then she said, "What? That's not nice."

"What's not nice?" Rachel asked.

"Maggie, the love of my life, the reason I get up in the morning, mainly because she gets up so freakishly early, just said that I should stick to American accents. Midwestern ones, preferably."

Rachel laughed. "I think she's saying you have no range."

"The hell with both of you all. I'm only marrying her because she's so damn cute. And the grin she just gave me confirms this."

Rachel laughed. "Yeah, have you started planning that yet?"

"Actually, yes. We're mostly done."

"Wow, already? When were you going to tell me?"

"When we were done. But, sure, now's good too."

"But how can you be done already? Don't weddings take months to plan?"

"Not for us. We are very simple people. We already have a cool spot picked out to get married in. Not going to tell you where yet—I want it to be a surprise. We're both wearing suits, if you can imagine. Of course Bill will stand with her. Dix is getting certified online so he can marry us. It was his idea. Since neither one of us is religious, we definitely didn't want to go that route."

"That's it?"

"Yep, that's pretty much it. Just got to worry about the food and get invitations. Simple stuff."

"Aren't you forgetting something?"

"Nope, can't think of anything." But Rachel heard merriment in Rory's tone and knew she was lying.

"Rory Morgan, I'm going to give you to a count of ten to tell me I'm your best person or I'm hanging up this phone. Ten, nine, eight—"

"Duh, of course you are. Geez, no one else could ever embarrass me like you, so of course you get the job."

Rachel squealed in triumph.

"Ow, don't squeal in my ear like that."

Rachel stopped and said sheepishly, "Sorry. So does this mean I get to wear a suit too and make a toast?"

"Yes on both accounts. Just don't embarrass me too much. I know where your bodies are buried, Rachel Cole, and I have pictures."

"Nonsense, I always make sure there's no photographic evidence. Can I bring Bobby?"

"Of course you can. I know he's part of the package now and I'm happy for you, Rachel. And so is Maggie—she told me to tell you."

Rachel felt herself blush and hated it. Rory was the blusher, not her. "This could be the one, Morgan. This could be it for me."

"Oh, it's natural to think that after the first time." Rory snickered.

"Oh, shut up! When I said it to you it was literally and truly your first time and my point still stands."

"Maybe for some people, but I still think I'm in love with her."

"You better. I really want to wear this suit. Talk about a first time."

"You'll look cute in it, I gotta admit."

"Aww. Thank you."

"You're welcome, now I have to go. That much sentiment made me nauseous."

"God, I know, douche."

"Right back at ya, ho."

Bobby was enjoying the few hours in his day before he had to go to work by sitting completely dressed in jeans and T-shirt, sock footed on his brother's couch, eating a bowl of leftover spaghetti he had brought home from work the night before.

The restaurant he worked at didn't just sell pizza, they had a full buffet with several different Italian staples, and the workers were allowed to take some home at the end of the night. He didn't care that it was only ten in the morning. Who made the rule that said certain foods should only be eaten at certain times of the day, anyway?

He had the TV tuned to *The People's Court*, not because he had a passion for the law, but rather, a passion for the hot Latina judge who thought nothing of rattling something off in Spanish anytime one of the litigants said something completely stupid and she just couldn't hold back her incredulousness any longer. He didn't get to watch her every day but he relished it when he did, and it was a secret passion no one else knew he had, as his brother worked first shift and he had yet to share this secret with Rachel. He figured she would understand.

He was halfway through his bowl and the judge was halfway through tearing into some poor soul who didn't bring enough evidence to support his claim when there was a knock at the door. Bobby put his bowl on the coffee table and muted the TV before he got up to answer. When he opened it, he was surprised to see who was on the other side.

"Mom!"

She seemed surprised as well and she took in his condition at a glance. He could tell she had sized up the situation accurately in that one glance, had noticed that he was in his socks and his hair wasn't combed.

Finally, finding her voice, she said, "What are you doing here?"

Bobby gulped, momentarily taken aback by the abruptness in her tone and the fact that after two years he was finally face to face with his mother. Then he realized that she should have known Chris was working. "What are *you* doing here?"

"My *son* lives here. I have every right to be here. And you never answered my question."

Realizing there was no point in lying, he said, "I live here."

"Figures. Your brother always did have a heart for strays. He was always bringing in one rangy mutt after another. I guess you're the latest."

Trying to control his anger, Bobby said, "Yeah, guess so. Chris isn't here, he's at work."

"I see. Well, I just wanted to make sure he was coming for dinner this Sunday. Tell him to call me." She started to walk away.

"Why don't you just call him?"

She hesitated. "You know I've always preferred face-to-face communication. Why should I call him when he's only on the other side of town and I had other errands to run anyway?"

"You knew I was here, didn't you?" Bobby crossed his arms over his chest as he leaned in the doorway. His mother wouldn't look him in the eye.

Finally, she said, "Yes, I had heard from Mrs. Jackson across the street. She goes to my church, you know? She said she thought she saw you here but wasn't sure. Said you looked so different. Said you looked like a boy, for crying out loud."

"I am a boy, Mother, remember? I'm not trying to look like one. I thought you knew that by now."

"No, you're not!" Bobby's mother looked around herself sheepishly, then stepped closer to him. "No," she said, her voice lower, "you most certainly are *not* a boy. You were born a girl and that's that. I know, I'm your mother. I was there when they put you in my arms." There were the beginnings of tears in her eyes when she said, "They put the most beautiful baby girl in my arms. I looked into your eyes and said, *There's my Emily*. And you smiled at me, like you recognized the name." Her expression grew hard. "But this"—she indicated Bobby's body and attire by waving her hand down the length of him—"this is not my daughter. I don't know who this is."

"I'm your son, Bobby. You have two sons, Mom. You always have."

"No! I only have one son and his name is Chris. You are not a son of mine. You know what the bible says about wearing opposite-gender clothing? It says—"

Bobby cut her off. "Yes, Mother, I do. And I'm not wearing opposite-gender clothing. But I also know what the bible says about denying your relatives and loving one another. You taught me that. Don't make me use your lessons against you. I always thought love was patient and kind, Mother. Or is the bible wrong about that too?"

"The bible is never wrong. And don't you dare quote the Lord's word against me! You're the one going to hell, not me."

"Is that what you came here for, to tell me that? You've told me that before. Next time you come, try to say something different or don't come at all." With righteous anger, Bobby slammed the door in her face, then slid down to the floor with his back to the door, brought his knees up, and covered his face with his hands.

He didn't give in to the tears, he never did. He just rubbed his eyes and took a deep breath, then let it out slowly. Why, why couldn't she just accept him as her child? He didn't understand where her vehement hatred came from or why he let it get to him so much. He knew he would never be able to accept her for the way she was, any more than she could accept him. They were at an impasse and neither was budging.

"I don't need you!" he hollered, letting out a child's plaintive cry of defiance, but he felt better once he said it. He didn't know if she was still outside or not, but he hoped she still was and that she heard him. "Just let me be!"

He wiped his eyes before any moisture could fall from them and betray him. He took one more deep breath, let it out, then pulled his phone from his pocket and sent Rachel a text. *Want to help me blow off work?*

You, blow off work? That's new. But okay, sure. You okay?

I will be when I see you. I need to see you.

Sure, baby. Can it wait an hour? In class right now.

Okay. What building? I'll pick you up.

Rachel told him where she was and he told her he'd see her in an hour then put his phone back in his pocket. He glanced at the muted TV and said, "Sorry, Marilyn, our date's off. Maybe another day." He sighed at the TV, then got up from the floor and turned off the TV before picking up his bowl of forgotten spaghetti from the coffee table. "Dammit, and that was good spaghetti too. Now it's ice-cold. Just like my mother's heart. At least this I can warm up."

Chuckling to himself, he went back into the kitchen to re-heat his meal.

❖

"I'm so sorry, baby. I wish I could make it better." Rachel lay holding Bobby to her chest in her bed.

She'd brought him there after he picked her up from class and she saw the state he was in. He had bravely given her a smile but she hadn't bought it for a second. Once in her room, she had taken his face in her hands and said, "Tell me."

So, after sighing, he had put his hands on her hips, looked at the floor, and told her about his mother's visit. When he wouldn't look her in the eye, as if he was ashamed of the whole thing, Rachel put her arms around his neck and her cheek to his and sank into his arms as they encircled her waist.

She kissed his neck softly and said, "It's okay. It's okay." Then she had led him over to the bed and pulled him to her chest, where he lay against her now as if she was his only port in the storm.

"You are—making it better, I mean." He snuggled closer to her and soaked up her warmth, taking in her scent, which was something light and floral and reminded him of spring. He breathed it in and sighed happily. He could feel the tension leaving his body as Rachel held him and stroked his hair.

"I'm just so sorry you had to go through that. I wish I had been there."

Bobby chuckled against her chest. "Why, so you could threaten her with all that kung fu you know?"

Rachel laughed easily with him. "Maybe. She wouldn't have known the difference. I would have done what I had to do. Nobody hurts my Sweet Boy." Rachel kissed the top of his head and Bobby smiled into her neck.

"You're like a lioness protecting her cubs."

"You're not my child—and thank God for that, let me tell you, don't need that psychological minefield. But you are most definitely mine and don't you forget it."

He leaned his head back so he could look up at her and they shared a smile. "No, I definitely won't forget it. Why do you think I'm here?"

Rachel gave him such a loving smile, and then she started singing something soft and slow. When she was done, he reached up and kissed her on the lips.

When he pulled away, she said, "You like that?"

"Ah, Rachel, I think you could sing me to sleep. And I mean that in a good way."

"I'll take that as a compliment. You want to nap? You want me to sing for you, baby?"

"I don't know. I didn't come over here just to nap in your bed. How rude would that be?"

"No, you came here because you needed me and I'm here for you. And if you need me to sing to you, I will."

"You do have a lovely voice. Maybe you should be pursuing music and I should be going to your classes."

"Nah, not for me. I just like to sing. I don't want to pursue it professionally. If I can sing for you and it makes you happy, then that's enough."

"Everything about you makes me happy, Rachel. I just want to lie here with you, forget the rest of the world, and listen to your heartbeat. Is that okay? Can that be what we do today?"

She caught her breath. She felt so many things just then but none she could give voice to. Finally, after a moment, she said, "Yes, baby that can be what we do today."

She kissed him sweetly on the lips, lingering just a moment with his bottom lip to remind him that she was available for whatever kind of comfort he needed, but she wasn't insistent and when he didn't return the passion, only the sweetness, she backed off and just continued to hold him, sighing contentedly. Then, she began to sing to him again, a favorite by The Pretenders this time.

Rachel reassured him over and over again that she would stand by him. She hoped he knew that her words were true and that she meant it every time. She felt his body relax and become more at peace as she continued to sing. This was where he belonged, and she hoped he knew that.

She felt the tears that must have rolled down his cheek because they dampened her shirt when he turned into her more and buried his face in her chest. She tightened her arms around him, and there was a catch in her throat, but she finished the song just the same. When she was finished, she leaned his head back and kissed both of his cheeks, kissing away the tears, then placed a small kiss on his lips. Without a word, she sat up just enough to pull off her shirt and throw it onto the floor. Then she pulled him back to her bare chest, and he put his face to her bare skin and kissed her hot flesh tenderly above her heart.

She whispered, "You're mine and I'm not going to let anyone hurt you." She stroked his head and his lips found their way to her nipple and he began to lightly suck on it. She arched her back to give him better access, and he began the slow caress of her body with his fingers and lips and tongue.

CHAPTER NINE

B obby sat at his brother's kitchen table the next morning, nursing a large mug of coffee and trying to ingest some eggs, to help boost the testosterone he injected once a week. He had agreed to work an earlier shift today so that he could be off sooner and spend more time with Rachel. He wasn't used to being up when his brother got up and usually missed the frenzied dance his brother did from his bedroom, to the bathroom, back to the bedroom, to the kitchen, back to the bedroom for that thing he forgot. It amused him and also always shocked him some-what to see his brother dressed for work. His brother worked in a bank—doing what, Bobby wasn't quite sure—which meant he wore a suit every day and carried a soft-sided leather briefcase. When he saw him like this, Bobby had to remind himself that this was the same guy who used to go mudding on the weekends and who had a closet full of camo clothing.

Bobby shook his head. He didn't understand his brother but he was a good guy.

Chris came into the kitchen, set his briefcase in a chair, and tousled Bobby's hair. Bobby grinned and smacked his hand away.

"What are you doing up so early, little brother?" Chris asked, as he was pouring his travel mug full of coffee.

Bobby swallowed and said, "Fuck off."

Chris threw back his head and laughed. "Such language, little brother. So, anyway, how'd it work out with the hot blonde of yours?"

Bobby smiled and nodded. "It's good."

"Ah, good, glad to hear it. I knew it would work out." They fell silent as Bobby ate his eggs and Chris sipped his coffee. Finally, Chris said, "So, Mom called me. Why didn't you tell me she came by?"

"Sorry. It was a bad experience, as usual. I just wanted to get away from it. Sorry, I should have told you."

Chris took a seat at the table. "How bad was it?"

Bobby nodded. "More of the same. She only has one son, I'm going to hell, I'll always be her little girl. Same ol', same ol'. I should be used to it by now, right?" Bobby attempted a smile but it faltered and he shifted his gaze from his brother's eyes to the table.

"No, you shouldn't be used to it!" The vehemence in Chris's voice surprised Bobby, but in a good way. "This is her fucking problem, not yours. You're who you've always been. Only now, as an adult, you can finally fully express that. She needs to work on getting over this if she wants to keep you in her life. Someday, you're going to look really different and she's not going to recognize you at all."

"Yeah, and that would be bad how? Maybe when I have facial hair and no tits, she'll finally be able to see me as a man. Or not. She may never come around."

"Look, I know she's our mother and it's natural to want her to accept you. I get that. But try not to expect it. I'm not saying you do, just, you know, don't expect too much from her. I don't know if she's ever going to change."

"I know. I just don't see why she came over here in the first place, if it was just to tell me the same thing. What satisfaction did she get out of that? I mean, does she enjoy making me feel like shit?"

"Maybe. Or maybe, in her own way, she's doing what she thinks is best. Trying to save you from eternal damnation or some shit."

"Are you defending that nutcase?"

"No, I'm trying to understand that nutcase. And accept her for who she is."

"Don't lecture me about that, Chris. How would you feel if she didn't even recognize you as her son? Totally dismissed you. Turned you into persona non grata."

Chris sighed. "I know I can't wear your shoes. I am secure in the body I was born with and the world accepts me that way. So no, I can never know what it's like for you, no matter how much I love you and am on your side. That's a privilege I know I have. The last thing I'm going to do is tell you to forgive her and ignore her behavior. I just wish there was a way you two could find peace. This way is not good for either of you. Or me. She's pissed at me now."

"Sorry, man. I didn't mean for that to happen."

"Not your fault. And Dad's just as bad. He backs up everything she says."

"Of course he does. He's afraid of her. She bosses him around, always has. Not that I'm defending him. He's an asshole too."

"Yeah, well, it runs in the family, I guess. I gotta get to work." Chris stood up from the table and pushed his chair in, then picked up his briefcase and coffee. "What's your girlfriend's name?"

Bobby tried to suppress the grin but couldn't. "Rachel."

"You going to see her later?"

"Yeah, planning on it."

"Well…give her a big sloppy wet one for me." Chris grinned.

"Get out of here before I put egg yolk on that pristine white shirt of yours." Bobby loaded his fork with egg and made as if to fling it at his brother.

"Ouch, harsh. Now that hurts. Fine, I'm going. See you later, little man."

Bobby just grinned to himself as his brother left the kitchen.

❖

Later that evening, when Bobby got off work and Rachel's classes were done for the day, they were walking around the duck pond, hand in hand. Every once in a while, Bobby couldn't resist stopping her for a kiss. It made her smile every time. He loved how her eyes seemed to shine when she smiled, and the look she gave him seemed to be filled with the same unexpressed emotion he felt.

"Rachel, has anyone ever told you that you're wonderful?"

"All the time. It's become such a cliché anymore." She grinned at him and squeezed his hand.

"Oh, I see. I guess I'll have to come up with something better to call you."

"That's okay. You don't have to call me anything—just keep calling me."

"Yeah, I don't think you're getting rid of me at this point."

"Really? Obsessed with me now, are you?"

Bobby threw back his head and laughed. "Definitely."

"Damn, it was the singing, wasn't it? Did I lure you from your ship into the ocean? Have I made you drown?"

"Yeah. And I don't want to be saved." He stopped her again, released her hand and put his hand on her waist, and kissed her.

Rachel reached around and moved his hand to her ass and their kiss broke into soft laughter. Bobby left his hand where she put it and leaned his forehead against hers.

Rachel sighed. "What am I going to do with you?"

"What do you want to do with me?"

"Mm, dirty, dirty things, my boy. Dirty, dirty things."

"That sounds nice, but I think we need to find a better spot than this."

Rachel encircled her arms around his waist and hugged him tight. "All things in time. I think I'm going to make you wait awhile. Make you squirm. Make you beg."

Bobby groaned and Rachel chuckled evilly and pressed her breasts to his chest, just to torture him, he was sure.

"You enjoy that, don't you?" he asked.

"Oh, I do, I definitely do."

"As long as you still want me, I can't complain."

Rachel looked at his face and gave him a stern but affectionate look. "Of course I still want you. In fact, you're so permanent in my life that you're taking me to a wedding in the spring."

"I am? Who's getting married?"

"Rory and Maggie, I told you that. You're my plus-one. I'll be wearing a suit and looking fabulous, of course. I mean, I haven't seen the suit yet, but how could I not?" She grinned at him.

"I'm sure you will. So I guess that means that if I want to look as good as my hot girlfriend, I have to wear a suit too. I haven't had occasion to wear a suit yet. This'll be fun. Thank you for inviting me, Rachel."

"Oh, this isn't an invitation. I'm just telling you where you're expected to be."

"Oh, I see. Of course, I will be wherever you think I need to be."

"Mm, I can picture it now. You're going to look so damn good in a suit. You're going to outshine the brides, who are also going to be in suits," Rachel mused.

Bobby laughed. "A lesbian wedding with my lesbian girlfriend, and I'm a trans guy who's never worn a suit before. Doesn't get any gayer than this."

Rachel laughed with him. "The only way it would is if RuPaul showed up and sang them down the aisle to 'Sissy that Walk.'"

"Wouldn't the other one, the one about being jealous of his boogie, be more appropriate, considering what you said happened here before they left?"

"Oh my God, yes, that's perfect! I'll have to tell them!"

Bobby looked nervous once their laughter died down. Rachel got concerned and put her hands on either side of his face. "Baby, what is it?"

"Do they know about me?"

"That we're dating? Yeah."

"No, I mean…"

"Oh, yeah, of course. You have to know, I tell Rory everything." Bobby raised an eyebrow in alarm. "Well, not everything, some things I keep to myself. But yes, they both know and they are supportive. They love me and only want me to be happy. If I vouch for you, you're as good as in." Rachel gave him a small smile and caressed his cheek.

"Okay. I just don't want this being awkward for you."

"No, it's not going to be awkward for me. Will it be awkward for you, being around my friends? My *real* friends?"

"Maybe a little, but that's something I have to get over. What if I have a beard by then? I've been on T now for several months and by the time of the wedding it'll have been about a year. I could have facial hair by then. Won't that look weird to them? Seeing you with someone with a beard, I mean?"

"Wait, we never discussed this. You want facial hair?" Rachel eyed him cautiously.

"Well, it's probably going to happen whether I want it to or not."

Rachel expelled a breath. "Okay, that's true. I can't be selfish about this, though I want to. Do you want a beard?"

Bobby shrugged. "I don't know. A lot of guys let them grow to help cover up their girlish face until it starts to hollow out. Also, I just think some guys feel manlier with facial hair."

"Do you feel that way?"

"Not really, you know? But I think I might want a beard just for the sake of it. Don't worry, it would be kept trim and neat." He grinned at her.

"Oh God, don't tell me I'm dating a hipster! Anything but that!" Rachel threw back her head in mock horror.

"Rachel, you met me in a lesbian-owned coffee shop. How could you not know that about me?"

"What can I say, I was concentrating on other things," she said seductively.

"Oh, like what?"

"Like how hot the blues singer was."

"Oh, really?"

"Yeah. The only thing that mattered after that was getting his attention."

"Well, you did. And you still have it."

"Good. Now walk me back to my dorm and let me show you just how much you have *my* attention."

"My pleasure."

"Not yet, but it will be."

❖

Mumbling to himself, Bobby said, "It's about me, not about you, that's what she had said." He quickly wrote that line on the notebook resting on his knees. He was sitting on his brother's sofa, in jeans and a white sleeveless undershirt, what Rachel called his butch look. When he had insisted he didn't think the word butch applied to him, since he wasn't a lesbian, she told him that lesbians didn't own butch.

Thinking of Rachel made him smile and he tapped his pen against the notebook as he continued to think. He scribbled some more, scratched something out, stared off into space, and then hit with inspiration, leaned forward to write again. Occasionally, he would sing a line out loud, pause, sing it again with a word change, shake his head in satisfaction, then write it down.

Chris came in and sat next to Bobby on the couch. "Whatcha doing, little brother?"

"Nothing. Just trying to get something out of my head." He wrote something else down.

Chris peeked over. "I haven't seen you write in a while. Glad to see it. Rachel's influence?"

Instead of acknowledging his brother's words, Bobby said, "What are you doing here? It's Saturday, shouldn't you be getting dirty or taking Marissa somewhere?"

"Mudding has lost its appeal and Marissa's working today. I'll see her later. What about you? It's your day off. Why aren't you making out in some dorm room right about now?"

"You think that's all we do?"

"Actually, I try not to think about it. But for your sake, I hope so."

"Why do you care if I get laid?"

"'Cause it means you're not being a moody little asshole on my couch."

"Fuck off."

"Oh, your comeback—it burns!" Chris feigned pain and Bobby narrowed his eyes at him.

"Anyway, in case you haven't noticed, it's fall break. She's spending it with her family. She won't be back until next week." Bobby knew he would miss her but he also enjoyed his alone time. Plus, she promised to call him every night and regale him with stories about the Crazy Coles, as she called her family.

"That sucks. Now I have to put up with you."

"You trying to kick me out? You want to bring Marissa over or something?"

"Oh, I'll bring her here whether you're here or not. That doesn't bother me. I don't give a shit." They were quiet a moment, and then Chris said, "I really am glad you found Rachel. I was tired of you whoring around."

Bobby narrowed his eyes at Chris, trying to suppress his anger. "Whoring around? That's what you think I was doing?"

"Hell, Bobby, you were like a kid in a candy store. You brought so many people home, I stopped asking for names."

"Which I was glad of, after that one mistake you made."

"Not my fault you were fucking people with similar names. After that, I either ignored them or just nodded. Not like they were going to be around long enough for me to care. I'm just glad you seem to be settled now. I'm a little surprised you're dating a lesbian, considering your luck with them in the past, but not for me to judge on that. I haven't met Rachel, but you seem happy and I'm glad. You little shit."

"Thanks, asshole. Besides, Rachel's different. I mean, at first, she had some issues to get over, about her own identity, you know? But she never put it on me, never made it seem like her questioning herself was in some way my fault. She actually felt guilty about it. No one has ever done that before. The other lesbians I've known got pissed at me because I made them question things about themselves. Rachel's not like that. I don't think she wanted to hurt me." Bobby felt his face flush at the revelation of so much emotion and he looked down at his notebook and pretended to cross out a stray word, but really, he rewrote the same word on top of the old just to give himself somewhere else to focus his attention.

Chris coughed, maybe to cover his own embarrassment. "Well, good. I look forward to meeting her. I just wish you could patch things up with Mom."

"Patch things up? It's not like we had a difference of opinion. She can't accept me for who I am and that's just unacceptable."

"You're right. I'm not defending her, just saying I wish things were different. This sucks."

"You're telling me."

"But I guess I'll just go on being the favorite until she stops being a bitch. 'Bout time I get to be Mom's favorite. It was tough living in your shadow." Chris said it with humor but his smile faltered a bit.

"What can I say? Doesn't matter what gender I'm displaying, I'm still the cute one. What's not to love?"

"You're an ass—always have been, always will be."

"Just trying to keep it consistent."

"Whatever. Let me hear that when you're done," Chris said, indicating the notebook, before he stood up from the sofa and left the room.

Bobby smiled and shook his head. He pulled out his phone and sent a text to Rachel. *I hope you're having a good time. I miss you.*

I miss you too, Sweet Boy. It's crazy here. Wish I could see your sweet smile.

Bobby grinned, then turned the camera on and took a selfie, something he normally didn't do. He sent it to Rachel with the message, *This smile is only for you. Keep it safe.*

You're a dork, Bobby Layton, but an adorable one.

Bobby couldn't keep the grin off his face as he set the phone down and went back to work on his writing.

❖

"Then my dad said, *Why doesn't that hot redheaded friend of yours come by anymore?* And my mother was like, *Maybe she got tired of you leering at her like you always do.*"

"Your dad's a letch?" Bobby was lying back on his bed later that night, listening to Rachel's stories. She had a way of making the horrible sound humorous.

"Oh, yeah, always has been. I mean, he's usually discreet about it to the point only Mom and I notice. Rory never has. At least, she's never said anything about it to me."

"Can't imagine that'd be an easy thing to talk about. Has he come on to your girlfriends before?"

"No, because he's never met them. I make sure of that."

"Honey, I'm sorry you have to deal with that. That's shitty."

Bobby could almost hear the shrug in her voice when she said, "I'm used to it. At least both my parents accept me as I am. Now that's shitty."

Bobby got quiet. "Yeah, I'm used to it."

"You shouldn't have to be though. Expecting your child to be who you think they should be, then getting pissed when things just don't work out that way? It's about control, plain and simple. She wanted to have control over your life and hates that she can't."

"I never thought of it like that before. I just thought she was a bible thumping bitch."

"Well, I can't speak to that." That made Bobby smile. "But I know not all parents come around. Rory told me that her future mother-in-law refuses to meet her because she can't handle Maggie being gay. Totally different from Rory's parents. They're awesome people. They pretty much adopted Maggie on sight, apparently. Me too, really. But there's no accounting for taste."

"I think it shows good taste."

"It's okay for you to say that—you're besotted with me. But *I* can't say it without sounding egotistical."

Bobby laughed out loud. "Can't argue with any of that."

"You would be wise not to. I really do wish there was something we could do to get her to come around." Her voice had turned serious. "But I know we shouldn't force it, either."

"Yeah. It'd be good if my dad wasn't a wimp but I don't see him changing." Bobby sighed and ran his hand through his hair.

"It'll be okay, baby. Hey, parents aren't everything, you know? So we weren't blessed with the best parents, who the fuck cares? They don't control our lives. We make our own way in this world. Whether we succeed or fail from here on out, it's up to us. What do we need them for? Okay, I need them to pay my college tuition, but besides that, not a goddamn thing. They can all just suck my dick, for all I care."

Bobby couldn't stop himself from laughing out loud and holding his sides. "Oh my God, you're awesome. I love you." He threw the words off casually, not fully realizing what he had said or the impact the words would have until Rachel went silent. "I mean, I, uh—"

"It's okay, I know what you meant."

Recovering, Bobby said, "So, um, tell me more about your family. Despite your dad being a letch, they gotta be better than mine."

"Oh, I guess they are in some ways. When you put the whole leering-at-my-friends thing aside, he's not a bad guy."

They talked some more, making each other laugh, both steering clear of anything that might hint at the word Bobby had casually let slip out.

After hanging up, Bobby, still smiling, picked up the notebook from his nightstand and began to scribble again, rocking back and forth the whole time to the tune in his head.

CHAPTER TEN

The following week, when Rachel came back from her parents' house, she called Bobby and said, in no uncertain terms, "If you don't get your sweet ass over here in ten minutes, I'm going to have to find another hot pizza delivery person to warm my bed."

Bobby rushed over to her dorm, and when Rachel met him at her door, before he could open his mouth to say anything, she had her arms around his neck and her tongue down his throat. When she finally pulled back for air, she said, "God, I missed these lips."

With his arms around her waist and a smile on his face, Bobby asked, "Only my lips?"

Rachel played with his hair and echoed his smile. "No, of course not, just especially." Rachel removed herself from his embrace, then grabbed him by his belt buckle and pulled him into her room.

He grinned slyly at her and as soon as the door was closed behind him, he pulled her to him and attacked her mouth just as furiously as she had attacked his. She couldn't help but chuckle some at his urgency.

Bobby rested his forehead against hers, his arms around her waist and closed his eyes. "I'm glad I didn't have to work tonight." Suddenly, he hesitated, as if not sure how to say what was really on his mind. He stole a glance into Rachel's eyes, then studied her smile. "I just, I want...I..." He blushed adorably, but then he broke his gaze with her again.

Rachel put a hand to his cheek and caressed him there. "Shh, it's okay. I know. Me too. Come on." She stood back and took him by the hand and led him to the bed, where she gently pulled him down next to her and she put her arms around him and gave him a soft, gentle kiss on the lips. She whispered, "Don't tell me, show me."

Thinking he might suddenly start crying at her gentleness and thinking how unmanly that would be, Bobby hid his face in her neck, where he first began by kissing in the hollow between her neck and her shoulder, very lightly. Then he moved up to her ear, the whole time his fingers softly exploring her body, not yet removing the barrier of their clothing, just enjoying the sweet, slow exploration. When she moaned against him, it excited him, sure, but it also made him want to take it slower, enjoy every inch of her, extend her pleasure.

They spent the next several hours in such peaceful repose and occasional slumber that a few hours later they were lying peacefully in each other's arms. Bobby was almost asleep when he sat up in bed with a start.

"Fuck, I almost forgot about the gig tonight. Shit, I have to go." He frantically began looking for his discarded clothing and binder and began to get dressed.

Rachel, splendidly naked beside him, sat up more slowly and asked, "What gig, baby?"

"The one at the café. They're having a benefit tonight for Al's sister's cancer fund. I told them I would sing tonight. You want to come?" Bobby stood up to pull his jeans up and buckle his belt, then went on the hunt for his shoes, finding one under her bed, the other kicked across the room under Rachel's desk. He retrieved them and sat on the desk chair to put them on.

Rachel gave a mock sigh. "You mean, put clothes on and leave the room?"

Bobby grinned. "Personally, I don't care if you're naked, and Tiff and Al might enjoy it also, but I can't speak for everyone. Besides, you might get chilly."

Rachel stood up, walked over to him and pulled his face to her bare belly. He kissed her there. "You could keep me warm," she said seductively.

Lost in the moment, Bobby put his hands on her hips and began a slow kiss up to her right nipple. Rachel put her head back and moaned as Bobby's lips found purchase and he began to suck her breast into his mouth. Rachel swayed forward and Bobby's arms went around her and her fingers entangled in his hair. Bobby was about to trail his fingers down to her wetness that he knew was waiting for him, but pulled away, since he knew they didn't have time to start again.

He kissed her above her heart and smiled and said, "We have to go, but I promise to finish this later."

With her fingers still entwined in his hair, Rachel yanked his head back playfully and said, "Oh yes, we will, yes, we will. But it was cruel of you to get me so worked up just before we walk out the door."

"All part of my evil plan to leave you wanting more."

"Hmm, well, it's a good plan." She sighed and backed away. "Okay, I guess I will cover this fine body with clothes, all for the purpose of being seen in public with you. You better sing a song for me." Rachel backed away and started to retrieve her own clothes that had been scattered hither and yon as Bobby had undressed her.

"We'll see, we'll see."

Rachel sat at the same table as the night when she had first seen Bobby up on that stage, singing the blues. She felt foolish now for thinking at the time that he was a dyke. How stupid she felt. She still wasn't quite ready to let herself off the hook for that one. She couldn't take her eyes off him as he conferred with the house band about the songs he was planning to sing. She smiled to herself when she noted how rumpled his clothes were, having been haphazardly and quickly discarded earlier in the day. She also knew that if he were to take off the long-sleeved shirt he wore unbuttoned with the sleeves rolled up, everyone would be able to see the large hickey she had given him just above the neckline of his undershirt. She bit her lip at the memory of the salty taste of his skin and the way he had moaned when she was leaving her mark, the way he had put his hand on the back of her head to push her farther into him.

Every time he let her touch him she took as a gift. Not that he was stone, but she knew he had some areas of his body that still required extra care, and as his barriers melted away little by little, she felt all the more protective of him.

"Mind if I share your table, or do you have people coming?"

Rachel turned around to see a tall brunette at her table smiling at her and indicating the extra chair at her table. She was a stranger to her, but it was a packed house and Rachel had no use for the chair at the moment. She smiled. "No, go ahead."

"Thank you." The newcomer pulled the chair back and sat, placing her glass of ice water on the table. "I really wish I could have a beer right about now."

"I know, but I've gotten used to it."

"Come here often? I'm sorry, that sounded like a cheesy pickup line. I didn't mean it that way." The girl smiled in her embarrassment and extended her hand. "I'm the incredibly embarrassed Melanie."

Shaking her hand, Rachel laughed. "Nice to meet you. I'm the easily amused Rachel."

"Nice to meet you, Rachel. My question still stands, though with innocent intentions."

"And my answer, also innocent, is that yes, I do. The entertainment's good. And the atmosphere." How easy it would be to pick this girl up, if she was still so inclined. She was cute, funny, and adorably awkward. Kind of like Bobby. But that thought led to thoughts of him and she couldn't stop herself from glancing over her shoulder at him and smiling.

Melanie, apparently thinking Rachel's comment was only referencing Bobby, snorted and said derisively, "Don't waste your time."

Rachel had to tamp down her sudden anger at the tone of Melanie's voice, when she asked, "What do you mean?"

"I thought he was a lesbian, but he's not, as I'm sure you can tell by my pronoun choice. He's trans. I mean, he's adorable, don't get me wrong, and one hell of a kisser, but, ugh, it was such a disappointment, know what I mean?"

"I'm not sure I do."

"Well, you know, I only date women, and I thought he was one. If I had known the truth, I wouldn't have let him make out with me in my car and I sure as hell wouldn't have let him get as far as he did. Just wish he had been honest with me from the get-go, you know?"

Swallowing her growing rage, Rachel asked, "So what, you expect him to just say, *Hi, my name is Bobby. I'm trans?* Because that seems a bit unnecessary to me."

"Well, maybe not like that, but he could have still let me know before I got naked. I mean, how rude." Melanie gave a crooked smile, as if to suggest her words were all in good fun, woman to woman.

Rachel was not finding amusement in her words at all. "I see. And how did you handle the situation when you did find out?"

"I told him to get the fuck out of my car, for one. Then I called him a liar and, well"—Melanie leaned closer to Rachel as if she was imparting a secret, and lowered her voice—"I called him a lying tranny faggot. I know it was horrible but I couldn't help it. That's how he made me feel. I think he'll think twice before he lies to another woman again about who he really is." Melanie sat back with a look of satisfaction on her face, almost, Rachel thought, like she thought she had performed a public service.

She couldn't hold back. The word tranny really pissed her off. She leaned toward Melanie and lowered her own voice, which forced Melanie to lean in to hear. "If I ever hear you say anything like that about my boyfriend, or any other transgender person again, I will fucking kill you, you stuck up little bitch. Now get away from my table." Rachel leaned back and cocked on eyebrow expectantly. Melanie looked as if she had been punched and Rachel got a great deal of satisfaction out of that.

Recovering, Melanie said, almost inexplicably, considering the harshness of Rachel's words, "Bobby's your boyfriend?"

"Yes. And you're sitting in his chair. Now leave."

"Whatever. You two deserve each other."

"Thank you."

"If you're a lesbian, as I suspect, considering how you looked at me when I first walked up, then you're a traitor—I hope you know that," Melanie said, as she stood up from the table.

"Why, because I'm not dating a lesbian? I prefer to date a person, not an orientation."

Melanie gave a derisive snort. "Whatever. Have fun with the dickless wonder up there." She walked away with a little wave.

Rachel exhaled and unballed her fists that she had clenched some time ago, though she couldn't remember having done so. Once she felt she could breathe normally again, she turned her attention back to the stage just as Bobby was approaching the mic. She was so glad he hadn't witnessed the exchange she had just had.

"All right, let's start off tonight with a sweet little Bill Withers tune." The music started and Bobby went into a soulful version of "Ain't No Sunshine." When that finished, he amused everyone by seguing into The Temptations and singing about "My Girl." Then he kicked up the sex appeal a notch with "Mustang Sally," but touched Rachel's heart when he left no doubt that he was singing directly to her when he sang "Stand By Me."

As he sang to her it was easy to forget the horrible conversation she had just had and it made it possible to concentrate on what really mattered: that sweet boy onstage who needed her to be strong. When he finished his set, she blew him a kiss and he caught it in the air and held his hand to his heart. It made her sigh, but just the same, she mouthed to him, "You big dork," which made him laugh.

When he finally left the stage, the first place he went was to her. She kissed him, then whispered in his ear, "Damn right I'm your girl and I definitely stand by you. And yeah, I forgive you for being a jerk." Bobby looked confused at first, then he nodded his understanding.

Rachel rapped her knuckles on Dr. Silver's door, being careful not to spill the coffee she carried. She had a cup in each hand, so the only other option for knocking would have been her elbow or her foot, but that would have been too awkward.

"Come in," came Dr. Silver's soft-spoken voice from inside.

Rachel was grateful the door was cracked, so she only had to push it open with her toe. She poked her head in and smiled. "Columbian, skim milk, with a dash of maple syrup, right?" She held one cup aloft toward Dr. Silver.

Dr. Silver looked up and smiled. "That's right. Since when does our campus coffee shop offer maple syrup?" She took the cup and carefully made a place for it amongst the papers on her desk.

"They don't, but the fast food place next to it does." Rachel took a seat without being prompted.

"Good to know. So, unless I miss my guess, the coffee tells me you are here to seek my wisdom." Dr. Silver leaned back in her chair, hands clasped casually across her lap.

"Not really, more like an update. I'm sure you were just dying to know."

Dr. Silver grinned but deadpanned, "I've been on pins and needles."

"Figured as much. Thought I'd come and set your mind at rest."

"It's about time. So how are things with…Bobby, was it?"

Rachel smiled. She could tell Dr. Silver noted it but didn't remark on it. "Well, I got over most of what we talked about last time. I mean, what you said made sense. I just had to realize that I know who I am and the hell with what anyone else thinks."

"Absolutely. I'm glad. So you resolved your other conflicts?"

"Other conflicts?" Dr. Silver said nothing, just raised an eyebrow. Rachel caught on and felt her face get hot. "Oh, *those* conflicts. Yeah, I have." Rachel grinned. "It's all good." She held her hand out, palm down, and moved it across the air as if across a flat, smooth surface.

"I figured it would all work itself out."

"Yeah, you're like an all-seeing guru that way."

Dr. Silver gave a surprised laugh. "I don't know about that. It is said wisdom comes from age, when in fact, it comes from making mistakes, usually stupid ones. I suppose I've made enough to be considered wise in that respect."

"How much wisdom you got about former hookups?"

Dr. Silver snorted. "If the subject was ex-girlfriends, quite a lot, but since I don't do hookups, none in that respect. But I'll do my best. What's on your mind?"

"Well, before Bobby and I met, he dated and screwed around a lot. So did I, if truth be known, so I can't fault him for that and it really doesn't bother me. The problem is that I ran into one of his former hookups at the café last night when he was performing. She didn't know we were dating when she sat down at my table. She proceeded to tell me, a total stranger, about how they hooked up but he was a total disappointment because he was trans and she thought I was mooning over him and was trying to tell me to not waste my time. I mean, what a douchey thing to do, you know? First, to out him as trans to someone she didn't know just cause she was pissed was really shitty, and then what she told me she did to him *because* he's trans? That was unconscionable."

"I see. I've never had this experience, so I don't know that I have any particular wisdom on this."

"Okay, maybe asking for wisdom wasn't the best way to put it. I think I need a different type of help."

"Such as?"

"Can you teach me that fancy kung fu you know?"

"Technically I can and do teach others on the weekends, but why? You're not going to start kicking the snot out of all his hookups are you?" Dr. Silver grinned at her.

"No. Though about his mother, I make no promises. No, but last night's incident and my reaction to it just made me think about other things that could have happened. I mean, she was a total bitch and full of bitterness but she wasn't violent. What if things had gone differently though? Things are getting crazy out there for trans folks. Scary, actually, and I want to be prepared. I'm not saying I'm looking to start fights or that he wouldn't be able to take care of himself if it came to that, just that I don't want to be the sniveling little chit crying at his side. I have a mouth that can get me in trouble, and now I need the skills to cash the check. And yes, I know I just mixed my metaphors and I don't care." She grinned to cover up her sudden nervousness.

"You're right about the state of things and the violence and hatred. And the whole bathroom thing is just stupid." Dr. Silver sighed.

"Exactly. And it pisses me off."

"Me too." They said nothing for a moment while Dr. Silver eyed Rachel levelly, and Rachel stared back unflinchingly.

Finally, Dr. Silver exhaled and said, "Okay, I'll teach you. Mondays, Wednesdays, and Fridays, four p.m. That is, if you will be patient with my teaching methods and let me do my job." Her tone was light and Rachel knew she was only teasing.

"Okay, since you're going to be teaching me cool things, I promise to be good. Can I wear the cute little pajamas like I saw you wear in the video?"

Dr. Silver did not smile and Rachel suddenly felt chastised when she said, "The uniform you saw me wear was called a *sahm* and I think you'll be fine in sweats."

"Aww."

"All things in time, young Padawan."

"That was a *Star Wars* reference, wasn't it?"

"There may be hope for you yet, Ms. Cole."

"Thank you, Obi-Wan."

"I think you should stop while you're ahead, grasshopper."

"All right, I'm going. Thank you."

"You're welcome. And congrats on Bobby and thanks for the coffee. It's always welcome."

"My pleasure. See ya, Lou." Just as she was about to walk out the door, Dean Louden appeared in the doorway. He had his hand raised in position to knock on the open door and he looked somewhat confused and taken aback. Rachel wasn't sure if it was because he had heard the nickname she had used or just the fact that she was there in the first place.

"Miss Cole, is everything all right here?" He eyed both of them in turn.

Rachel turned so he couldn't see her and rolled her eyes at Dr. Silver before turning back to look at him again. She patted him on the arm and said, "Relax, Charles, it's all good. Just student/teacher business, honest. Besides, she's cute and all, but not my type. No worries."

"I'll see you in class, Ms. Cole," Dr. Silver said. There was no mistaking the stern tone in her professor's voice, which Rachel took to mean, *Shut up and go now*.

"Right. Gotta go. You should relax more, Charles, it's good for you. Bye, Dr. Silver, and thanks for all the fish." It was fun to exchange geeky references with Dr. Silver. She'd been missing this kind of banter since Rory moved away.

"Anytime."

As Rachel was walking away, she heard the dean ask, "So what was that about?" She sighed and hoped she hadn't just gotten the prof in trouble. Obviously, he was still a little nervous after the whole Maggie and Rory thing. Was it not possible that a student and teacher could be friends, or whatever it was that they were, and for there to be nothing between them? She was amused at the thought that Rory had just ruined it for everyone. She made a mental note to tease her about that later.

CHAPTER ELEVEN

So, I'm curious—why can't you see me this afternoon?"
Bobby called when he woke up on Friday morning to
say that his boss had changed his shift to that evening, which
meant he wouldn't be able to come by, not that they had any
specific plans. He had asked if he could spend the afternoon
before shift with her instead as he'd done many times before,
but Rachel was simply vague and said that she had other plans.

"Because, I told you—I'm going to a workout session. It's a
new thing I've started. I'm sorry I can't see you before work, but
I can wait up for you." She dropped her voice into a seductive
whisper to try to make up for disappointing him. She wasn't sure
why she didn't want to tell him about the kung fu lessons, other
than the fact that she was a little embarrassed. Maybe she would
tell him someday, she reasoned, when she actually had something to show him. There had to be a move that would lay him
on his back. She smiled as she thought it, realizing she didn't
need any help in that area.

"My shift ends at midnight. That won't be too late?"

"I'll be here. And awake. I promise."

"Okay. If you're sure it's okay. Just so you know, I'm not
going to smell my best."

"Hmm, too bad I live in a dorm with a communal shower.
Otherwise, I'd throw you in there and wash it all away."

Bobby groaned. "You're torturing me. And you're enjoying it, aren't you?"

Rachel laughed. "Maybe."

"Evil, just evil."

"You wouldn't have me any other way. You love it."

"You know I do."

Rachel's voice softened. "And don't worry, I really am working out. I'm not blowing you off. Trust me, if I could be with you more often, I would."

"I'm not worried. I trust you, Rachel, more than anyone."

Rachel couldn't help but put a hand to her heart. But instead of telling Bobby that, she reacted with her usual humor. "Aww, right in the feels."

Bobby laughed. "That was my goal. I'll see ya later, Rachel."

"Bye Bobby." Rachel hung up and sighed. "You're being a goofy, grinning idiot, you know that, right?" she chastised herself. With another sigh, she picked her phone back up off the bed where she had laid it and sent Rory a quick text, realizing as she did so that she hadn't spoken to her all week. *Goddammit, I'm falling for that big dork. That's all.*

A minute or two later Rory's reply came back. *Aww. I'm happy for you and that big dork. Congrats! It's about damn time!*

Yeah, yeah. She chuckled to herself as she set her phone back down on the bed then stood up to change into sweats and a T-shirt. She wasn't sure what exactly she was in for today, but she had a feeling Dr. Silver was definitely going to be putting her through her paces and she was most assuredly going to get a workout.

Dr. Silver had told Rachel to meet her in the same multipurpose room their stage combat class was held, promptly at four o'clock. When Rachel had left her room it was ten till the hour and she had to jog in order to make it in time. Something about her professor's tone told her that she had better not be late.

When she finally pushed open the large black door to the rehearsal space, it was two minutes after the hour. Not bad, she thought. Dr. Silver was standing in the center of the room, looking as patient as you please, with her hands clasped in front of her, her honey-blond curls pulled back, her glasses held on with a strap. She was wearing the same black and red outfit she had worn in the video she had shown in class, the one she had referred to as a *sahm*. The desks that were usually scattered about the room in a haphazard way were all neatly lined up along the side of one wall. There were mats in the middle of the floor, the same ones that were used in their stage combat class. It was on one of these mats that her professor stood.

Rachel walked up to her teacher, palms together at her chest, and bowed. "Sorry I'm late." It seemed like something she was supposed to say. When she looked up again, she thought she saw Dr. Silver suppress a smile.

"Accepted. The bow is not necessary, but if you wish to do so, this is the proper way." Instead of palms together as Rachel had done, Dr. Silver put her hands down at her sides and then bowed.

"Oh, sorry." Rachel copied her movements.

"Yes, like that. In this room, during these sessions, you will refer to me as *Sifu*, not Dr. Silver or Lou. You will be on time. You will not wear jewelry or street shoes. You will do everything I tell you and you will bow to me after each instruction, when you step onto the mat, and before you leave it. If you find that you do not wish to continue, then you will inform me of this instead of only giving half the effort. What you are about to undertake is not easy. It requires a lot of endurance and strength and commitment. This is a skill that, once mastered, will be with you a lifetime and can be very rewarding.

"In order to do the movements Wushu requires, it is important to have flexibility. There are a number of different techniques I will show you that will help your body move in the ways it is supposed to move, but first we must start with dynamic stretching. You have to wake the body up and make sure it's ready to move. If not, you can suffer injuries. Follow my lead. Try to copy these as best you can."

Dr. Silver then proceeded to show Rachel a series of kicks that definitely stretched out the legs but were more elegant than any stretching Rachel had ever done. They looked more like ballet moves.

Rachel wasn't sure if she could even get her leg up that high. "Are you kidding me?"

"Am I smiling?"

Rachel gulped. "No, Sifu." She bowed the proper way this time, but then became curious. "I have a question, Sifu."

"Yes?"

"Why these types of stretches and not the regular ones?"

"Because, over the last several years, it has been found more beneficial to do the standard types of stretches—which are called static stretches, by the way—at the end of the routine. This type of stretching is more helpful to do at the beginning because it activates the muscles we're going to be using and is more of a full-body warm up. Any more questions?"

"No, Sifu." Rachel backed away to find a better starting point, then did as told. She had already gotten a little sweaty on the jog over, as the fall weather had yet to fully take hold and was still warm and humid. After a few not so graceful kicks, her shirt started to cling to her in some places, and the back of her neck was starting to get wet. Rachel wasn't sure how many kicks or types of stretches she did, could have been five, maybe more, when Dr. Silver stopped her.

"Okay, enough. Back over here. Consider that your warm-up."

"Yes, Sifu."

After the stretching came a series of jumps and kicks and weird hand movements that made Rachel feel she felt awkward and sluggish when she did them. But when she watched Dr. Silver's quick movements, she couldn't help but stare in awe. Dr. Silver moved her body swiftly and elegantly and with great purpose. Watching her in person was way better than the video, and Rachel felt lucky that Dr. Silver had agreed to teach her. And somewhere in the middle of it all, she realized that she just might enjoy learning kung fu just for the sake of knowing this beautiful discipline. By the time the session was over she was proud of herself.

They ended the session with static stretches, which Rachel recognized from grade school gym class. She trusted Dr. Silver knew what she was doing.

When the stretching was over, Dr. Silver announced, "All right, that's enough for the first day." She bowed to Rachel, who bowed in turn, and then she turned her back on Rachel and went to get a drink from the water bottle she had off to the side. The professor was only mildly sweaty, compared to Rachel, who was drenched in sweat and felt like Rocky after he had run up the steps of the Philadelphia Museum of Art.

Now that the session was over, Rachel felt the formal air in the room had been let out and she said with a smile, "Lou, you're kind of a badass."

Lou gave her a small smile and inclined her head. "Thank you. I have a black belt in badassery."

Rachel gave a surprised laugh. "Do you ever wear it with your *sahm*?" she teased.

"No, it's too big." Lou grinned, then threw Rachel a bottle of water. "Here. You need to hydrate. Next time, don't forget to bring some."

Rachel caught it with her right hand, surprising herself by not fumbling. "Thank you." She took a grateful gulp.

"Slow down, or you'll puke."

Rachel stopped drinking abruptly and swallowed what was in her mouth. "Thank you, good point." After she had taken another cautious sip she said, "You know, we never discussed payment. I have money. I can and should be paying you for this."

"No, what we are doing is informal. If you were to come to the school where I am an assistant instructor, then it would be right and proper for you to pay. For this, I will not take payment. It is my pleasure to teach you."

Rachel knew she was blushing. "Wow, thanks. But is there nothing I can do to show my appreciation?"

"Yes, actually, there is."

"Name it."

"Show up. Do all the things. Without protest. Learn."

"I will. I want to do this, not just for him."

"Glad to hear it. See you Monday." Dr. Silver made to leave and Rachel started to fall into step beside her. Dr. Silver stopped her. "I said it was informal but I still respect tradition. I leave first. Got it?" This time there was no mistaking the smile.

Rachel fought to keep her own smile at bay, as she instinctively knew that, while it was fine for her teacher to make any facial expression she wanted, even though they weren't in a formal session now, it was still improper for her to return the same. "Yes, Sifu." She bowed, as she knew she should and was already becoming habit. She just hoped she didn't bow to her in class. That would be awkward.

Dr. Silver left and once the door closed behind her, Rachel let out a breath, hugged her arms to herself in a stretch, and said, "Ow. Yeah, I'm gonna feel that in the morning." Then she made the long walk back to her dorm, knowing she wasn't going to be able to jog as she had on the way in, hoping she had the strength to get in the shower.

❖

Rachel wasn't used to that much physical activity all at once. Dancing for hours in her favorite club was about as physical as she got most of the time. Her muscles were definitely awake now, she thought, as she gingerly climbed into the shower. The hot water felt so good on her muscles, like a balm. She understood why there was a hot tub in the locker room for the athletes, the lucky bastards.

She stood under the water, letting it beat on her shoulders, wishing the shower had an adjustable head so she could make the water come out in a heavier rhythm. She stayed in as long as she could stand it, then turned the water off and stepped out into the entry area, where there were hooks on the wall for the hanging of towels and robes, and grabbed her towel, dried her hair as best she could, and then wrapped the towel around her body and left the bathroom.

Despite how much her muscles were talking to her, or maybe because of it in some strange way, she still felt wonderful, she had to admit. It felt good to know that she had it in her to do the things Dr. Silver was asking her to do, and she didn't totally suck at it. That was the amazing thing. She wanted to talk to someone about this and realized that other than Bobby, the only other person she ever wanted to share anything new with was Rory.

After she hung her towel on the towel rack in her room and then put on a pair of boy's boxers that she always thought she looked cute in, and a clean T-shirt, she lay back on her bed and called her best friend.

"Hey, Rachel. Good to hear your voice."

"You're sounding way too chipper for the occasion. Did you just get laid or something?"

"Why are you always so concerned if I'm getting some?"

"I am not! I was just pointing out that you are in an exceptionally good mood and usually when you get this way, you've just been with Maggie."

"What can I say, the woman makes me happy." Rory sounded very happy.

"Giddy is more like."

"Call it what you like. But for your information, Maggie isn't even here. She left this morning for some theater education conference in Boston. I had to stay here. I'm grounded."

"Aww. Did you pee on the rug again?" Rachel teased.

"No." Rory sounded forlorn. "I have a paper due on Tuesday and I know that if I don't spend this whole weekend working on it, it's not going to get done. So, sadly, I am home alone."

"So you were giddy when I called because you're sick of staring at a computer screen and were happy for any distraction?"

Rory replied, "Yes!" She sounded happy again.

"I see. Okay, I'll be your distraction. You know, you've never told me what that school is like."

"Small, it's small is what it's like. But, that being said, the teachers are pretty cool and there's that social justice group I mentioned. They're really more aware of social justice stuff up here, so there wasn't any awkwardness about us being gay. And Maggie's coworkers, who know me both as a student and her fiancée, don't treat me weird or seem to talk behind our backs. They just accept us as a couple. The students too, really. Basically, no one gives a rat's ass what we do, and it's awesome."

"That does sound nice." Rachel sighed.

"It is."

"Can we talk about me now?"

Rory chuckled. "By all means."

"Okay. Well, I started doing something new that I can't tell Bobby about. I mean, I could, but I just don't know how to."

Rory asked, "Rachel, what have you done?" There was a note of warning in her voice Rachel had heard a million times before.

"Nothing! I mean, nothing bad like you're implying." Rachel lowered her voice. "I just started taking kung fu lessons." She waited to see if Rory would laugh but she did not.

"Interesting. What got you into that?"

"Dr. Silver. She's the new Maggie. She's a real badass and she offered to teach me. I mainly did it because I wanted to be able to fight bad guys, but I really enjoy it."

"Rachel, I had no idea you wanted to be a ninja. You learn this skill, you can be a real femme fatale."

"I only want to lure one male and I've already done that. Plus, I have no desire to bring him to his ruin. But I'll settle for ninja."

"As the kids say, you go, girl."

"Is that really what the kids are saying?" Rachel asked incredulously. "I don't think they're saying that anymore."

"Like I would know?"

"There's this thing called the internet—it'll teach you what people our age are into. You might want to read up on it."

"Who has the time? I have fifteen pages to write and I'm only on page four."

"Since when are you so behind on schoolwork? Aren't you the one that gets your papers done like a month before they're due or something?"

"That was before, when I had no life. I have a life now. And as you are often alluding to, I get laid. A lot. So priorities, innit?"

Rachel laughed. "Yeah, I know what you mean."

They talked for another hour or so. When they finally hung up Rachel looked at the clock and sighed. How was it possible that she felt this exhausted and it wasn't even nine o'clock yet? She'd promised Bobby she would be awake when he showed up and she meant to keep that promise. She looked at her desk and saw her stack of books and remembered the homework she had due for Monday, grateful that, unlike Rory, she didn't have a paper to write, just reading. A lot of reading.

Resigning herself to her fate, she got up and took the top book off the pile, which happened to be the book for Dr. Silver's class, then checked the reading assignment. Fifty pages. Not bad. She took the book with her to the bed and, after adjusting the pillows for a better sitting position, sat down to read. She figured she would finish that in a couple of hours at most and she could move on to reading for another class and possibly even get most of her homework done before Bobby even showed up, which would mean more free time.

She scooted down on the bed some so that she was practically lying down, but she forced herself to stay awake. She'd told him she'd wait up for him and she meant it.

❖

When Rachel didn't answer after a minute or so of knocking, Bobby tried the handle and found it unlocked. He had gone into her room once before in the same manner under the same circumstances—he had worked late and she had left her door open in case she fell asleep before he showed up. He figured that was the case this time and that she wouldn't mind if he came in.

He quietly opened the door and stuck his head in and saw her on the bed, fast asleep, with a textbook open beside her. He gently closed the door behind him, went over to the bed, and carefully leaned over her to take the book away. He set it on the desk. She didn't stir. Silently, he took the backpack off his shoulder, kicked his shoes off, then unbuckled his belt, slid his pants to the floor, and pulled his shirt and binder and bra over his head and added them to the pile. Then, clad only in his boxers, he lay down behind her and pulled the covers up over both of them, put his arm around her waist, and kissed her on the neck. Only then did Rachel react.

She turned around in his arms and draped an arm over him, snuggling into his chest. "Mmm, pepperoni. My fave."

Bobby chuckled. "Good," he whispered. "I thought you were going to stay up for me."

She mumbled, "Long day."

"I see that. It's okay. Is it okay if I stay?"

Suddenly more alert, Rachel pulled her head away and looked into his eyes. She touched his face. "It's always okay."

"Okay." All the times he had come over before, he had never spent the night, always leaving after a few hours, feeling like a thief in the night. That had never bothered him before with anyone else he had ever been with, but being with Rachel was different. He wanted to spend all the time he could with her. For once, he wanted to wake up next to someone and see them in the morning.

He kissed her then, but not in passion, not in invitation, only in promise. He touched her face and brushed the hair away, and they said nothing. Their legs entwined together and Bobby whispered, "Good night, Wild One."

Rachel whispered back, "Good night." Her hand came to rest on Bobby's chest and she closed her eyes.

Bobby smiled in the darkness but lay awake for some time afterward, just holding Rachel while she slept, trying not to disturb her.

CHAPTER TWELVE

The next morning, Rachel woke up alone. Her cover was down to her waist where it always ended up by morning and she was still in the shirt and boxers she had put on after her shower. She started to worry that she had dreamed that Bobby snuck in in the middle of the night, when she noticed he was sitting at her desk, with his back to her, fiddling with something she couldn't see. Something about the almost furtive nature of his movement stopped her from calling to him. Instead, she watched him.

After a moment, he put his head back and held something aloft, to better see it in the sunlight, she supposed. It proved to be a syringe and bottle of medicine. The needle was in the bottle and the bottle was upside down and a clear liquid was filling the syringe. She watched as he withdrew the needle, capped it, set it on the desk, then opened a small foil packet and began to clean a spot on his upper thigh with the wipe. When he was done, he set the used wipe on top of the foil packet, retrieved the needle, uncapped it, set the cap aside, then pinched a section of his thigh between his fingers, and with great purpose, injected the needle into the spot he had cleaned. Very slowly he released the liquid inside. Then when he was finished, he recapped the needle, put a Band-Aid on the spot, then zipped the needle and vial up in a small case.

Only then did Rachel dare breathe. Her exhale drew his attention and he turned around and gave her a small, shy smile.

"Good morning. I'm sorry for this." He waved a hand vaguely over his needle case. "Saturday's just my shot day. I can't miss it."

Rachel removed the blanket and sat up and ran a hand through her hair. "I hate shots." She shuddered. "Does it hurt?"

"Only if I do it wrong. Which happens sometimes." He shrugged.

"What do you mean?"

"If I'm not careful and push the needle in too fast or forget and put the shot in the same spot as last time. Which is part of the reason I have to switch locations from one week to the next. But for the most part, it doesn't really hurt. I'm tough." He gave a crooked smile and a half-hearted flex.

Rachel returned his smile.

Bobby grabbed his backpack off the floor and began to put his kit away, then pulled clean clothes out and began to change. Rachel stood up with a stretch.

"Seems a shame to cover up that gorgeous body." She went up to him as he was buckling his belt, took his hands off the buckle, and held both ends in her hands. She used the belt as a handle to pull him to her for a kiss. When she pulled away, she whispered, "Now why would you want to go and do a silly thing like get dressed, when you can stay naked and let me touch you, hmm?" She kissed him again and this time his arms went around her.

When he pulled away, he said, "Because it's easier for you to undress me if I have clothes on."

"Rather enjoy that, do you?"

"Mmm, much."

"So you weren't trying to run out the door?"

"Why would I want to do that? Except to pee. I've been putting it off. The men's floor is so far away."

"One floor is far?"

"It is when you have to piss this bad."

"You have such a way with words."

Bobby looked down. "Sorry. That was kinda gross."

Rachel lifted his chin, forcing him to meet her gaze. She leaned in close to him and whispered, "If you have to piss, go piss." She pulled back. "Well, you might want to put a shirt on first though, but don't do it for my sake."

Bobby laughed. "Okay. Then maybe we can go out and do something."

"Fine." She stood back from him. "Now go. I have to make myself gorgeous for you."

"You already are. I've never seen you in boxers before. You look really cute."

"That's what I was going for." She smiled at him, and then walked over to her dresser while he reached down to the pile of clothes he had discarded the night before and pulled his binder out of the mix.

Rachel watched him. The binder he had worn the first time they'd slept together had zipped up like a vest, but this one was different. This one was beige and wrapped around his chest like a bandage and Velcroed on the side. The end result was a flat, more masculine chest. Under an undershirt and a T-shirt no one was able to tell it was there. Rachel just couldn't imagine the pain he must endure—all for the sake of appearances and peace of mind.

As she pulled on a pair of jeans, she cocked her head. "Hey, baby, why don't I go stand guard at the girls' bathroom like the straight girls do for their boyfriends? Not something I thought I've ever have to do, but, whatever." She shrugged.

"You sure?"

"Yeah. You're no different than those jerks. Okay, as I was saying it, I knew it was wrong. You *are* different than those jerks. You're a sweet boy and you don't smell nearly as bad as they do."

"Are you talking about the pepperoni smell or the boy smell?"

"The boy smell. I hope that the longer you're on T won't mean the smell will get worse." Rachel crinkled up her nose.

"Not sure. I've read that it might go away once my body adjusts to the hormones and I level out. Of course, since I haven't had a hysto, I still have all these unnecessary girl hormones swimming around in me and they fight with the T, which means mood swings and bad smells. I'm sorry for both." He shrugged sheepishly.

Rachel went up to him and touched his face and gave him a light kiss on the lips. "Baby, I was only teasing. I'm sorry. It doesn't really bother me." She hugged him.

"Are you sure? You can tell me."

"Well, okay. I mean, you usually smell real nice and I love your cologne, but once in a while, you do kinda smell like a boy and"—she sighed and looked down for a moment—"it's kind of a turnoff."

"Hey, don't feel bad. I know you're not attracted to men and me smelling like one can't be good for you. I get it. You know, science says we are attracted to someone by smell. It's all about the hormones, baby."

"Is that what it is? You mean, it's not this hot body or those luscious lips?"

"Nope. That's just window dressing. Gives our eyes something nice to look at while the rest of our body is reacting to the smell."

"Well, I prefer what I'm seeing right now." She kissed him again, pushing herself against him, causing him to moan. After a moment, he pushed her away.

"Baby, I gotta go. Come on and be my lookout."

"Okay. Come on."

They went out into the empty hallway. It wasn't noon yet and Rachel figured most of her floor mates were still sleeping.

She walked to the bathroom down the hall, gestured for him to wait outside, then went in to check if anyone was in there. The coast was clear and she waved him in, taking her place outside the door so she could catch any of her neighbors before they went inside.

No sooner had she taken her place next to the door than Lori had opened her door and came sleepily out into the hallway, dressed in what Rachel knew she always wore to bed, an oversized old shirt with their school logo on the front that she had taken from Rachel when they had been sleeping together. Rachel didn't know why she still kept it; it was starting to look raggedy and worn. Lori glanced at her but said nothing.

"You can't go in yet."

Lori stopped in her tracks, looking confused. "Why not?"

"Bobby's in there. Give him a minute."

"You let him use our bathroom? Aren't there rules about that?"

"Yeah, that the bathroom has to be guarded, which I'm doing."

"No, I mean, shouldn't he be using a gender-neutral bathroom or something or just go upstairs?"

"There is nothing wrong with him using this bathroom. Eddie uses this bathroom all the time." Eddie was the boyfriend of one of the straight girls who lived on their floor. Rachel had seen Stephanie standing guard many times.

"Yeah, well, that's different."

"Seriously? Did you just seriously say that to me?" From behind her, Rachel heard the toilet flush, then a moment later the running of water.

"Yeah, you know why. Bobby's not like Eddie and you know it."

"No, you're right, he's a completely different human being. Good eye."

"You know what I mean, he's—"

Lori was interrupted by Bobby coming out of the restroom. "I'm what?"

Lori started to stumble in her words. "I…you're…just get out of my way."

Bobby stepped aside and Lori shouldered past him.

"How much of that did you hear?"

"All of it. This place echoes like crazy. It's all right. Nothing I haven't heard before."

"Well, you shouldn't have to hear shit like that." She raised her voice and directed it into the open bathroom door. "Some people should be fucking nicer!"

Bobby grabbed her by the arm and steered her toward her room. "Come on, Wild One, let's go get our wallets and keys and get out of Dodge."

"Are you trying to prevent a fight?" She directed her next statement into the bathroom again. "'Cause I could totally have taken her!"

"I'm sure you could have. Come on, we should probably go."

Rachel sulked. "You're ruining my fun."

"I'm sorry. Just trying to keep you out of trouble."

Rachel, calmer now, snorted. "I hope you're up for that challenge, dear boy."

"Working on it, Rachel, working on it."

"There's a reason I call you Wild One, and this is why." Bobby was laughing as he looked at her across from him on his brother's couch. After he had pulled her away from yelling at Lori in the hallway, they had quickly gotten what they needed from Rachel's room and left the building with no particular plans. Now that they were comfortable, he couldn't stop laughing.

"What? When someone's been a douche, I'm going to call them on it, that's all. I make no apologies." Rachel was reclining in the corner of the couch with her feet in Bobby's lap.

"Oh, I'm not asking you to. I just don't want you to put yourself in danger on my account." Though he smiled at her, there was a clear note of seriousness to his tone.

"Thanks, but don't worry about me. I'm mostly all talk, but I think I could hold my own if it came to it." She gave him a secret smile and pretended to bat her eyes at him.

"Yeah, I know, but still. I don't want to sound all harsh about it, but this isn't a joke. Harassment against trans folks is very real and can be very violent. I know, so far when we've been together it's just been your friends—"

"She's no friend of mine."

"Okay, ex-friend. But what if next time it's not? Baby, I love that you want to fight for me, I do, I just don't want you getting hurt doing it. Okay?" He tugged on her pants leg to make sure he had her attention.

She smiled in return. She could see how worried he was about her and she realized that it was time to tell him what she had been doing the day before. She sighed. "I'm not going to get hurt. Eventually, I'll even know how to fight back if it comes to that."

"What are you talking about?"

"The reason I was asleep when you came in last night was because of what I was doing earlier in the day."

Suddenly Bobby looked curious and suspicious. "What do you mean?"

Rachel scooted toward him until she was practically sitting in his lap and ran a finger across his jawline. "It's not what you think. I was with Dr. Silver." Bobby's eyes got wide and it made her laugh. "Oh God, no, that came out wrong. Not like that! I just meant that I asked her to teach me something outside of class that I thought might come in handy someday."

Bobby put his hand on her thigh and smiled. "And what would that be?"

"Kung fu."

"You are learning kung fu to protect me?"

"Well, at first. But I found that I kinda like it. It's fun."

"I see." Bobby looked down for a moment and there was a catch in his voice when he looked back up. "I don't know what to say. Thanks doesn't seem enough."

Rachel put her arms around his neck and kissed him. "It's okay. That's plenty." She gave him another kiss, this one softer and slower. His arms went around her and he pulled her closer to him.

"Oh, Jesus Christ."

Neither of them had heard the back door open and didn't know Chris was in the room until he spoke.

"This is not how I wanted to start my day." When Bobby and Rachel pulled away from each other, startled, there was a huge grin on Chris's face. "Well, hello, lovebirds. Why are you making out on my couch when you have a room of your own to do that in?"

"What are you doing here? Thought you were spending the day with Marissa," Bobby asked. Rachel scooted off Bobby's lap and went back to her corner.

"She got called into work. So I came home. Thought I'd spend the day with my baby brother. Get in some quality bonding time. But I see you're already bonding."

"Since when do you and I bond?"

"Oh, brother, I'm hurt." Chris sat on the arm of the couch next to Rachel. "Do you see how he treats me, his only brother? I don't know you, and yet I can sense you're too good for him."

Rachel grinned at Bobby then looked at his brother. "Maybe, but he's really cute. Good arm candy."

Bobby snorted.

"Okay, gross." Chris made a gagging noise.

"There wasn't anything gross about what I just said. What would be gross is if I started making out with him again." Rachel moved back to Bobby's lap. They both grinned at Chris. "I have no qualms about sticking my tongue down his throat again."

Bobby couldn't help but laugh. "Don't push her, Chris. She is nothing if not a woman of her word."

"I had that feeling. Thanks for making room for me." Chris sat down in the spot Rachel had vacated. Rachel, amused, put her face in Bobby's neck and chuckled.

"Can't you see I'm not in the mood to bond with you right now?" Bobby said.

"Can't you see I don't care? This is my house, little brother. My couch. Don't let me stop you from leaving." Chris picked up the remote control and turned on the TV.

Rachel stood up from Bobby's lap and grabbed him by the hand. "Come on, Sweet Boy, let's go make out in your room." Bobby stood up, still holding her hand, and made to follow her out.

"She calls you Sweet Boy? She obviously doesn't know you at all."

"Ignore him," Rachel said. "He's just jealous that you're about to get laid and he's going to have to wait until later."

"Oh yes, so jealous of my baby brother. What will I ever do?"

"Not much until later, apparently," Rachel threw over her shoulder as they were leaving.

Chris had a big grin on his face. "Hey, Bobby?"

Bobby stopped. "Yeah?"

"Good job." Chris inclined his head in Rachel's direction.

Bobby smiled. "I know, right?"

Rachel tugged his arm. "Come on, baby, you haven't shown me your room yet. I'll show you a good job."

"Yes, ma'am!" They were giggling as they made their way down the hallway to Bobby's room.

"Just try to keep it down."

"Bite me," Bobby hollered over his shoulder before he went into his room and closed the door.

"That's her job!" Chris yelled back just as the door was closing.

❖

"Do you think we have too much sex? I mean, there are other things we could be doing with our time, you know?" Upon asking the question, Bobby leaned in and gave Rachel a slow, lingering kiss.

"Sure there are, but why? We're young. This is what we are supposed to be doing. It's what our parents think we're doing, anyway. Do you want to be in your forties and think back to all the sex you missed out on in your twenties? I don't know about you, but I don't want to live in regret. Gotta take advantage of these hot bodies while we still have them."

"Couldn't argue with you there. Speaking of hot bodies, I was wondering something. Do you think your professor would mind if I came with you to a session? Kinda want to see you in action."

Rachel hid her face in the pillow for a moment so he wouldn't see her blush, then looked back at him with a smile. "It's hard to have a conversation with you when you say nice things like that."

"Really? That wasn't even that nice. It's not like I said anything about wanting to see how this perfect, compact body of yours looks when you're learning to be a ninja, or anything."

"Uh-huh, that's enough out of you for the moment. In an-swer to your question, I can't say—I'll have to ask. She might be okay with it but I really don't know. I get the impression that this is something she takes very seriously and follows tradition. I'm just not sure if it'd be proper. We'll see. I'll shoot her an email later. I should be asking why you would want to."

"You mean, besides seeing how sexy you must look doing this?"

"Of course, because that's always a given. What's your real reason?"

"Well, maybe I'm curious about this professor. Don't need you doing what your best friend did." He grinned and Rachel pretended to be shocked. She playfully smacked him on the arm.

"That was so not funny! And Dr. Silver is so *not* my type. She's too old and she's not butch enough for me. She's just a badass who's teaching me to be a badass. I could only hope to be that cool someday."

"I've always thought badasses were sexy."

"They are, but honestly, I just can't see her that way. I look at her and all I see is a teacher, not someone to be attracted to. I mean, she's okay, I guess, but she's no Dr. Baskin, that's for sure." She wiggled her eyebrows at him.

"Just how many of your teachers do I need to worry about, anyway?"

Rachel rolled on top of him, forcing him onto his back, and straddled his hips, then leaned down with her hands on either side of his head. Her blond hair and her breasts fell in his face and Bobby put his hands on her hips and made to bite her nipple.

She playfully pushed his face away. "Stop that. And to answer your question, none at all. But if you're a good boy, I just might teach you a thing or two." With that declaration, she gave him a long lingering kiss and his hands started to explore again. She let them at first but then she grabbed them and stopped their progress and chuckled. "Not now. Later. Now you're going to take me to lunch. I'm starving for some reason. Time to get up." She climbed off him and stood up.

He groaned in protest. "You are so mean to me."

"Anticipation, my dear boy, is how I will keep your attention."

"That's not what keeps my attention." He stood up and put his arms around her.

"Oh?"

"You don't know?" She shook her head. "It's everything."

She sighed. "Dork." She put her arms around him and hugged him, her head to his chest.

CHAPTER THIRTEEN

After spending a relaxing weekend together, Rachel had emailed Dr. Silver to ask if Bobby could attend her Monday session. She was surprised when Lou agreed. Since Bobby was only going as an observer, he was still wearing his street clothes. Before they left Rachel's room, he teased her about her workout clothes.

"I've never seen you in sweats before. Very cute."

Rachel smiled and faked a curtsey. "You think everything I wear is cute, but thank you."

Bobby walked up to her and took the string of her sweat-pants in his hand, tugging on it a little. "I've always wondered what the string is for."

Rachel grinned at him.

He pulled on it a little more and she grabbed his wrist but came forward. "Ah, now I get it," he said.

"It has many uses. I always thought of it like a pull-start on a lawn mower."

"That works too."

"Get that look off your face—we have to go. I can*not* be late." She stepped away and grabbed his hand and led him out the door.

They left in plenty of time, but just the same, she quick-ened her pace just to be on the safe side. When they got to the room, she stopped him outside the door and said, "Okay, just so you know, you're going to see a different side of me in there. It might be weird for you. Just promise not to laugh." She looked nervously up at him and he smiled and caressed her cheek.

"Don't worry. I'm not going to laugh. I'm going to stare in awe."

Rachel exhaled, feeling somewhat better. "Of course you will. Okay, come on."

She opened the door, pointed to a spot on the sidelines where he could wait and watch, then stepped onto the mat, where Dr. Silver was waiting. Rachel bowed as before. Dr. Silver returned her bow.

"Hello, Rachel. How do you feel?"

"Ready, Sifu."

"Good to hear. Okay, we are going to start with the same dynamic stretching we did last time and that will continue for most of our sessions. Then we will move into punches and lastly technique. Depending on your progress and what I think you need at the time, this may change from one training session to the next. Okay, let's begin."

Rachel bowed and then began to do the exercises as Dr. Silver indicated. It didn't take her long to shift her focus from Bobby and just concentrate on what she was doing. The warm-up took about twenty minutes and included all manner of calisthenics, and by the time Dr. Silver announced they were moving on to punches, Rachel was soaked in sweat and went over to Bobby before the next phase of the session began for a drink of water. It felt like she was going to her corner after round one in a boxing match.

For all the simplicity of the warm-up, it was definitely intense, and she was becoming aware of her body in ways she never had been before. Since Friday, her muscles had definitely come awake and several different areas had made themselves known to her. Her glutes and arms were sore but her abs felt tighter. It wasn't as if she was terribly out of shape, but she hadn't been treating her body very well and she told herself that she was going to change that.

The session today was two hours long and by the time she gave Dr. Silver her final bow and left the mat to get more to drink, she was exhausted but strangely exuberant. She thanked Bobby for handing her the water and wished she had brought something to wipe the sweat off her face. Next time, she told herself. After drinking, much more slowly than she had after the first session, she asked Bobby, "So, what'd you think?"

Bobby grinned. "It was awesome." He leaned down and whispered in her ear, "You look hot, by the way."

"I am—overheated, that is." She took him by the hand. "Come on, I want you to meet Lou." She dragged him over to where Dr. Silver was standing drinking her own water and toweling herself off.

She smiled when they approached. "So, you're the Bobby I've heard so much about?"

Bobby looked at Rachel. "How much has she heard?"

Rachel felt her face flush. "Don't worry." She turned to Dr. Silver. "Yes, this is him. I swear I wasn't making him up."

Dr. Silver smiled and extended her hand. "Nice to meet you, Bobby."

"Same."

"What'd you think of what your girlfriend was doing today?"

"I thought it was really cool. What you can do looks really sweet. Are you a black belt or something?"

"I'm flattered. And to think, this isn't even my final form." She grinned at them. "I don't much care for rankings, but I have earned a black belt over the last few years," Dr. Silver said, somewhat demurely.

"Cool! So could you run a dojo or whatever it's called?"

"Wushuguan, and yes, if I wanted to, but I'd rather focus my attention on teaching theater. I like learning this discipline for its own sake and when I teach it to someone it's only because they really want to learn it. Like Rachel, here." She smiled at her and Rachel bit her lip. "She's a good student and I know she's going to continue to do well."

Bobby put his arm around Rachel's waist and beamed at her. "I don't doubt that. I was wondering…Would you be able to teach me?"

Rachel looked up at him, curious, but didn't say anything.

Dr. Silver took a moment to look him in the eye, just as she had Rachel, and gave a slow nod. "I can. Can you come when Rachel comes?"

"I'll make sure of it."

"Good." She turned to Rachel and said, "Just don't tell all your friends, since I'm not running a school here. I don't need a line of grad students thinking they're going to be Bruce Lee or an animated Jack Black."

Even though they weren't in formal session, Rachel bowed and said, "Of course not, Sifu."

Dr. Silver laughed. "I'm not sure if you were just being sarcastic there or not, but thank you."

"I'm not sure either, to be honest. Anyway, thanks, Lou. See you in class. Come on, I need a shower." She started to leave, then saw Dr. Silver's upraised brow and remembered, and stopped in her tracks. "Oh right, sorry."

Bobby, confused, asked, "What?"

"She goes first."

"Oh." Bobby stood to one side as Dr. Silver left.

Once she was gone, Bobby said, "Man, that was intense. The whole thing, not just that last bit."

"Are you sure you're up for it?"

"Baby, I am if you are."

"Why does that sound like an insult?"

Bobby laughed. "It's not, I swear. You want to go back to my place where we can shower together?"

"God, you're like a walking hormone."

"Well, yeah. What can I say, I'm a growing boy."

"Just exactly what part of you is growing right now?"

"I…" He couldn't continue because he started laughing.

"That's what I thought. Come on. We will *not* shower at your place. I will shower in my dorm, where you will wait patiently for me. If you're good, I might let you give me a massage afterward."

"Ooh."

"Stop that. Just a massage. That's the only kind of rubbing I want right now."

"Aww."

"Big baby." As she led him out, they were both laughing.

Once they had gotten back to the dorm, Rachel headed straight for the shower, and afterward, Bobby gave her a massage. While she was lying on her stomach, enjoying the feel of Bobby's hands on her body in a way other than sexual, she was compelled to say with a moan, "Oh, that feels so good."

"I'm glad. I haven't done this very often, you know?"

"Really? Well, it makes me feel special. Thank you so much. Mmm."

"Good, that's how you're supposed to feel, because you are."

"Aww, you're just saying that to get into my pants."

Bobby laughed. "You're currently not wearing pants. And it would be very easy for me to have my way with you if I wanted to. You are putty in my hands."

"Mmm, more like Jell-O. And don't be so sure about that. You only get as far as I let you get. I am perfectly capable of resisting you." Abruptly, she flipped over on her back and Bobby's hands ended up on her stomach. He grinned and playfully tweaked a nipple. Rachel did a sharp inhale but took his hand in hers. "Not yet."

"Okay. Whatever you say."

She smiled and sat up and pulled the sheet up to her waist, partially covering her nakedness. "Tell me something—why'd you ask to learn kung fu anyway?"

He pulled back and had a thoughtful expression on his face. "Can't I want to learn something new? I mean, it looked cool. Isn't that enough?" His tone had a sudden edge to it and he sat up more and moved away from her a little.

Confused at his sudden change in mood, Rachel said, "Yeah, of course you can. I was just curious." She looked at him for a moment then asked, "Is everything okay?"

He sighed and ran his hand through his hair. "Yeah, it's fine. Sorry, didn't mean to be a jerk about it. It's just a hard thing to talk about."

Rachel leaned toward him and touched his arm. "I'm not going to force you to talk about it if you don't want to, but I hope you know you can."

He gave her a wan smile. "Yeah, I know. Remember the other day when I said that violence against trans people was no joke?"

"Yes."

"I know because…I know because I've been jumped before. And I wasn't ready for it. I know the reality and I know if it happened once, it can happen again. I want to be ready for it this time." He shrugged. His hands were resting in his lap and Rachel took one of his hands in hers.

"I should have guessed it was something like that. I'm sorry for pushing you about it. I totally understand."

"You weren't being pushy, just curious. And you have a right to know everything about me. Some things are just harder to talk about than others, is all."

"I know." Rachel put her arms around him and held him close and kissed him on the neck. He returned the hug, holding her tight, and buried his face against her. She stroked his hair. They sat that way for a moment, and then he pulled away but stayed in her embrace.

With his forehead against hers and his eyes closed, he said, "It was a couple years ago. I was working for a sandwich delivery place in the city. It was dark." He spoke almost in a whisper, as if saying the words took all his energy.

Rachel interrupted him. "You don't have to."

"Yes, I do. No one answered the door, so I was heading back to my car when they jumped me. I don't know where they came from. Suddenly there were just three guys standing between me and my car. They called me a faggot and one of them was on me and held my arms, while another one started hitting me. The third one started smashing the windows out in my car. They kept calling me names and hitting me. At some point I just gave up and went limp. I just gave up." He stopped talking and silent tears wet his cheeks.

Rachel wiped them away.

"Shh. It's okay. It's over now. You're okay." She tried to put her arms around him again but he stayed rigid. He opened his eyes but couldn't look at her.

"All that kept going through my mind was Brandon Teena and Matthew Shepard and I thought they were going to kill me. They just wouldn't stop. Finally, someone walked by and saw what was happening and called them off and they ran. It was some older guy who lived in the neighborhood. He called the cops and stayed until they came. I never got his name."

He looked back up at Rachel and said the next sentence with vehemence. "My mother came to the hospital and said..."

He swallowed and Rachel could tell he was choking back tears.

"She said, *You shouldn't have provoked them.* That was the only thing she said. I shouldn't have provoked them. Then she left and never came back. My father just stood there the whole time shaking his head. I was living on my own but I got scared and Chris said I could move in with him. I don't want to be scared anymore, Rachel. I don't." He swallowed again and wiped his eyes. "I'm sorry."

"Oh, honey, why, why are you sorry? You've done nothing wrong."

"Because I'm not man enough. I don't know if I'll ever be." He looked down at his hands, which he had clasped in his lap. "I'm not what you thought I was."

Choking back her own tears, Rachel took his face in her hands and forced him to look at her. "You think being a man means not being afraid? You think I want you to be some clichéd behemoth who can't string two coherent sentences together but can crush beer cans on his head?" Bobby gave her a weak smile. "And, for the record, you are exactly what I thought you were. You're my sweet boy. But don't think because I call you a boy that means you're not a man. I call you Sweet Boy because you have a tender, innocent heart. I call you Sweet Boy because you put others before yourself and don't think twice about it. You can still be my Sweet Boy and be a man, just a different kind of man. Remember, I don't date men. That makes you special."

"I guess."

"Come here." Before he could protest, Rachel pulled him to her and leaned back on her bed and held him to her and stroked his hair and began to rock him back and forth very gently.

Very softly, he asked, "Can you sing to me?"

"What do you want me to sing?"

"I don't care, I just need to hear your voice right now."

Rachel kissed him on top of the head and said, "Okay. Shh. I got you." Then she began to sing, slow and soft. As she sang it became harder and harder to not cry but what kept her from sobbing was remembering the strong, sweet boy in her arms. She knew she had to hold it together for him. She would be strong for him.

❖

The next morning, Rachel didn't want to let Bobby go but he had to work the early shift again and she had no choice. Before he left, she stood with him at her door with her arms around him, just holding him close. Now that she knew what could happen to him, she felt like she was sending her baby to war and she hated it.

"Baby, if I don't go, I'm going to be late. You want me to come by after work?"

"I wish you could move in with me."

"I don't think the college would approve of that, since I'm not a student here anymore."

"I don't give a fuck what they think." She sighed. "But I know." She touched his cheek and kissed him one more time. "Can you text me throughout your shift?"

Bobby chuckled. "Yes. A little. I'll check in when I can. Rachel, that attack was two years ago. I'm going to be fine. But I'm glad you care so much."

"For *you* it was two years ago—for me it was last night. But I know." She put on a brave, fake smile. "Be safe. And get back here as quickly as you can, hmm?"

"Okay, I will, you have my word."

Sniffing back tears, she stepped back from him and said, "Okay, you should go before I tie you to the bed."

Bobby laughed and grinned. "Hmm, that could be interesting. Put that on the maybe list for later."

"Great, now I have to go shopping for restraints. Go on, get out of here." She waved him away with a smile.

"All right, I'm going. See you later."

"Duh. Now enough, go." With one last smile and wave, Bobby left. Once he was out the door, she covered her face with her hands and moaned out loud. She wished she could go down the hall, knock on her best friend's door, and drag her out to have a drink somewhere, not caring that it wasn't even noon yet.

Rachel missed Rory more than ever. She really could use a friend right now. She pulled out her phone and called Rory, not at all sure if she would answer. She knew Rory liked to sleep late when she didn't have a morning class but she had no idea what her current schedule was like. She just knew that if Rory was available she would answer. It took five rings, but she finally did.

"Rach?" She sounded groggy. "What are you doing up this early?"

"Bobby spent the night and had to go into work this morning."

"You okay? You don't sound right. Or are you just sleepy?"

"I'm *not* right. Did I wake you up? I'm sorry."

"Yes and no." Rory sounded more awake now. "I went back to bed after Maggie left. It's okay. What's wrong?"

Rachel sighed and collapsed across her bed. "Bobby shared something from his past last night. I don't know if I can handle this, Rory. I don't. This is scary."

"What is it, honey?"

Rachel started to silently cry again at the sound of love in Rory's voice and she wiped a tear away. When she spoke again she knew Rory would be able to tell she was on the verge of really letting go. She tried to swallow the tears as much as she could. "Something horrible happened to him a couple years ago. He got jumped by three guys. He was in the hospital for several days. They were stopped before they could do a lot of damage, I guess. I almost couldn't let him leave this morning, Rory. To think I have to let him loose in the world when there's people out there who will do shit like this just because he's different from them. I mean, I know that's the way the world is and it happens to a lot of different people. I just don't understand." Fuck it, she would let the tears come, let Rory hear her cry. This was why she called, wasn't it?

"Oh, honey, I wish I could be there for you. I can't hug you from this far away."

"It's okay. You answered, that's enough."

"I wish I had an easy answer though. As members of the queer community, we're all at risk, but him more than us, that's for sure. Look, I know you're scared for him and there's no way of knowing if it will happen again or not, though we all hope not. I think he's brave though, because he faces this kind of thing every day when he goes out into the world. It's gotta be tough to look beyond what did happen and what could happen and focus on the simple fact that, no matter what, he has the strength and the courage to face another day. He hasn't given up. It may have scared him shitless, and I wouldn't judge him if it did, but he's not hiding. He's living his truth every day. And all you have to do is care about him and cheer him on when things are going well, or hold him when they're not."

Rachel teased Rory through her tears. "God, did you change majors to psychology or something? You've become so damn analytical and insightful since you moved up to the Great White North."

"That's Canada, you dork."

"You're like a stone's throw away from Canada, so same dif."

"Thank you for proving that Americans still suck at geography."

"Hey, there's nothing wrong with my geography. I know where you live, Morgan. I can find you."

"Uh-huh. Come and get me, Shorty. I'm waiting."

Instead of returning the banter, Rachel turned serious again. "I know you are. Thank you."

"Anytime. Hey, Rach?"

"Yeah."

"You are free to visit if you want. You got plans for Thanksgiving?"

"Just my parents' house. Are you about to make me an offer I can't refuse?"

"Maybe. Maggie and I were talking about the holidays, and I was going to cook, of course. My parents are coming. Why don't you come up too? And if Bobby can get away, bring him."

"You have room for that many people?"

"Well, in truth, we only have one guest room and my parents are getting that, but I will always have room for you, even if it means on the couch, or if Bobby comes, the living room floor. It's what you do for family. You don't *make* room—there's always room."

Rachel felt like crying again but only because she felt so much love. "I'm going to say something to you I rarely say, so I don't know how you're going to be able to take it."

"Go ahead, I'm prepared."

"Good. You ready?"

"I said I was."

"Okay, here it goes…I love you, Aurora Morgan. Not in the same way I used to, but in a better way. You are the family I choose and I'm glad you choose me too." That was all. She couldn't say any more.

"I love you too, Rach. And I will always choose you, Pikachu."

"I am not a rodent, thank you very much!"

Chuckling, Rory said, "But you do have yellow fur and brown eyes."

"Oh, shut up. I'm hanging up now and I'll let you know about Thanksgiving. Jerk." She disconnected to the sound of Rory's laughter.

CHAPTER FOURTEEN

It had been two years since the bad thing happened. Bobby had long since healed. His body had, anyway. He had suffered a broken arm and a couple of broken ribs, both eyes had been blackened, and his face had looked like he had been in a boxing ring. He never forgot that it could have been much worse. It took him months to be able to sleep through the night without nightmares. He quit his job because he didn't like where his deliveries sent him—and anyway, he'd been sick of living in the city. He'd moved there when he dropped out of college, to pursue his music, but all he had been able to pursue was a delivery job and the occasional open mic. Nobody cared about his music, no one important anyway.

After the attack, he had admitted to his brother that he didn't feel safe in the city anymore and was thinking of coming home, but he was afraid of what their mother would say. Chris had said, "Fuck Mom. You're my brother and if I want you to live with me you can. She lives across town and never comes over. I have a spare room that I've been thinking of turning into a man cave, but you can have it until you can get your own place."

Bobby hadn't known what to say. He did something he rarely did—he hugged his brother and thanked him and said he loved him. Obviously embarrassed, Chris had returned the hug and the sentiment. Now, two years later, he was still in his brother's spare room, working another shitty delivery job, and still no one cared about his music. The only creative outlet he had was the local open mic scene. He wasn't sure what he wanted to do with his life with regard to his music, but now he knew that whatever he did, he wanted it to include Rachel.

He hadn't meant to tell her about the attack, at least not yet, maybe not ever. But she was so loving and so understanding, he knew he could trust her with it. He really did feel that he should be over the fear by now, and he was for the most part. Maybe, with her help, he could finally beat it.

He dropped a pizza off at a frat house, and since he was on campus, remembered to text Rachel. *Hey, just checking in.*

Thank you.

He smiled, then started driving back to the restaurant to pick up his next delivery. Rachel was the first relationship he'd had in two years. After he had moved in with his brother and his body healed, he had gone a little crazy, going out several nights a week, bringing a different person home every night. His brother had teased him about it sometimes, but Bobby knew Chris had been worried. Bobby wasn't even sure why he was doing it. It wasn't as if he could fuck his fears away but he had definitely given it a try. As he had told Rachel in the beginning, he had always been safe. He wasn't stupid. He enjoyed sleeping with both men and women and considered himself pansexual.

Chris had asked him once what *pansexual* meant.

He'd explained that he didn't really care about gender or gender identity or biological sex. He just wanted to connect with someone.

"And that's different from bisexual how?" Chris had asked.

"Well, it mainly has to do with gender identity and expression. Pansexuals don't care how another person identifies, whether male, female, trans, somewhere in between. Whereas someone who's bi usually assumes there are only two genders and may not date people in nonbinary categories."

"You kids and your hip lingo. In my day, you were either gay, straight, or bi." Chris had just grinned at him and Bobby knew he wasn't trying to be an asshole.

"That's because back in your day, you guys were too simpleminded to understand such things."

"Have you ever considered, little brother, that all these new words aren't necessary? Doesn't applying these labels sometimes make you feel like bugs under glass?"

"Only if that bug is a butterfly."

"Oh, that's girly as shit."

"This from the man with a teddy bear tattoo on his left ass cheek."

"You'd be surprised what you'll do for a woman, little brother."

"Too bad that woman dumped your tattooed ass. Anyway, butterflies are cool. They represent metamorphosis. They are one of the symbols of trans, you know?"

They had gone on like that, bantering back and forth. Even though Chris sometimes teased him about terms and other things about his gender identity that he didn't understand, Bobby knew Chris was the only one in the family who accepted him for who he truly was, even if he didn't understand exactly what Bobby was going through. The point was he was willing to learn about it and accept it.

On Wednesday Bobby accompanied Rachel to the training session in his own workout gear. He went through the same first day routine that Rachel had, including learning how to bow and where to stand. He took to the movements pretty easily and was enjoying himself. The only major problem he had was that his binder kept riding up or rolling under in uncomfortable ways and when that happened it was hard to concentrate on the activity at hand.

Unlike Rachel, who claimed she was not attracted to Dr. Silver in the least, he found her quite attractive. Not only was she cute, but she was fierce and he had always found that a heady combination. At least it didn't distract him so much that he wasn't able to concentrate.

He thought that, overall, he had been able to kick some serious butt during session and he liked the formality of the whole thing. It appealed to him in a way that working out with weights and swimming never had. Not only was he learning a new skill and getting toned in the process, but he knew that martial arts were meant to teach a person discipline and control, and those were two things he knew he needed to learn. Especially control. Rachel had never seen his temper before, as up to now he'd had no reason to display it, but he had been working on controlling his temper since he was a teenager.

He and his mother used to get into some massive screaming matches, which always ended in him throwing things and her quoting the bible at him. Once he started taking T, he knew it would probably make his temper worse, so he worked on ways to curb it. He had started meditating almost right after his first shot and that helped a lot, that and continuing to see his therapist.

He had initially started therapy because it was required to be approved to take T, but he had kept seeing her to manage the anger issues. He saw his therapist once a week and he still hadn't mentioned it to Rachel yet, even though, at this point, he figured she would understand.

When the session was over and he and Rachel had bowed to Dr. Silver, Bobby said, "Thanks, Sifu, for agreeing to teach me. You don't know what it means to me." Shyly, he inclined his head and almost missed Dr. Silver's warm smile of affection.

"My pleasure. And I think I have some idea of what it means to you. I'm just glad you're getting something out of it."

"Oh, I definitely am. Tell me something…how long did it take you to get this good?"

"If you mean my general skill level, several years. I couldn't put an exact number on it. If you mean my rank, around ten years. Becoming a master of your craft may seem like a slow process, but it's well worth it."

"I can tell. Why don't you wear your belt when you train us?"

"For the same reason I don't bring my diplomas to the classroom when I teach—they're only visual proof of my training and skill level and not necessary to do my job."

Bobby grinned despite himself. "But I bet it's a lot cooler than a piece of paper in a frame though, isn't it?"

Rachel narrowed her eyes at him and he wasn't sure why.

Dr. Silver smiled. "This is true. Rachel, I'll see you in class tomorrow and I'll see the both of you on Friday."

They exchanged bows, and this time Rachel apparently remembered not to leave first. Once Dr. Silver was out of the room, Rachel smacked Bobby across his chest with the back of her hand, though not too hard.

"Ow. What was that for?"

Rachel's amusement showed in the laughter in her voice. "As if you didn't know."

Amused and confused both, Bobby said, "I really don't know. Did I do my bow wrong or something?"

Rachel scoffed and shook her head. "Clueless male. If you really don't know, fine, I'll break all the rules of girl code and tell you. You were so flirting with her!" Rachel grinned at him and crossed her arms over her chest, then cocked an eyebrow, practically begging him to refute her.

"Wait. What? No, I wasn't. I was just genuinely curious, that's all." Despite his protests, Bobby could feel his cheeks getting hot and he felt caught. He had, in fact, found the professor adorable, but as far as he knew, he hadn't been flirting.

"Whatever. You are so obvious when you like someone. It's written all over your face." She went up to him and took his face in her hands and gave him a quick kiss, then backed away. "That's okay, I like that you're easy to read."

"I am so confused right now."

"Good, right where I want you. Come on." She sighed. "I guess now we *have* to shower at your place so that you can actually get a shower too."

They walked to the door hand in hand, and then she stopped him and leaned into him and said seductively, "If you're lucky, I'll make you forget all about Dr. Silver and I'll show you some new moves."

"Dr. who?" he asked, trying to be just as sexy, but Rachel burst out laughing and he wasn't sure why. "Now what?"

"Oh, nothing, I'll tell you later." She was still laughing as they left. Bobby was more confused than ever.

CHAPTER FIFTEEN

The week of Thanksgiving, Bobby was required to work every day except the holiday, as that was the one day that week that the restaurant was closed. He had wanted to go with Rachel to visit her friends. He knew how much it meant to her, but he needed the money and he couldn't pass up the hours.

Rachel had wanted to stay with him over the holiday, but he had insisted she go and just make sure to call him every night. He promised he would check in with her as much as he could during his shifts, but in truth he didn't want to intrude too much on her time with her best friend, so he didn't plan on texting her all that much.

As for Thanksgiving Day, his mother had planned her usual gorge-fest, to which Chris and Marissa had been invited, but not Bobby. Chris wanted to turn down the invitation but Bobby had insisted that he go. There was no reason why Chris should be on her shit list too.

Bobby tried to make it easy for him. "See, this way, you can go and bring back leftovers and she'll never know they're actually for me."

"Fuck, man, if I bring anything back, it's for me."

"Suck my dick."

"No thanks. Never cared much for the taste of silicone. But fine, I'll go home. Mom has been wanting to meet Marissa. Any message you want me to give her?"

"None that wouldn't get you smacked, not that I'm opposed to that, but it's a holiday, so…" Bobby shrugged.

Chris laughed. "Okay. Have fun. Sorry you're going to be alone on Thursday."

"I won't be alone. I'll have Snoopy and SpongeBob and more marching bands than you can shake a drumstick at."

"I think that was a pun."

"Probably."

So on Thursday morning, Bobby sat in his brother's living room, eating leftovers from work, watching the parade, his feet up on the coffee table, his phone by his side. Rachel had been texting him since she had gotten up that morning. She sent him a selfie with her best friend, who was gorgeous, but he knew enough to keep that thought to himself. He could see why Rachel had had a major crush on her. He was half in love just from the picture.

Before Chris left, Bobby made him stand still for a picture to send her in return, and his brother had timed it right so that he was kissing Bobby on the cheek just as Bobby had taken the picture. Bobby's look of surprise had been genuine. The caption he had sent it with was: *Make sure you tell them that I'm the good-looking one.*

The reply came back: *This is Rory. I thought you were the sweet one?*

Can't I be both?

Near as I can tell, you are. Keep it up and you just might win my approval, but I have to meet you before I can grant it fully. Christmas?

Will have to see how work goes. Maybe.

Bobby smiled to think that Rachel's best friend approved of him. He knew Rory meant a lot to her. He would have to be on his best behavior.

The next day, he was able to sleep in, as he wasn't required to work until the evening shift. He had agreed to work until close since Rachel was out of town. Besides, the tips were usually better at night, especially on a Friday after a holiday. Most of his money went for his treatment—he didn't have insurance, so had to pay for everything out of pocket and T wasn't cheap. At least his car was paid for, crappy as it was.

When Rachel learned that he was working the late shift again, she told him, in no uncertain terms, that he had to check in at least once an hour. It touched him, but at the same time made him feel guilty. He knew how troubled she'd been after she'd heard about his attack and he hated that he had put that worry in her.

So, dutifully, he checked in about once an hour. *Still safe. Still bored. What are you doing?*

The answer came back with a picture of Rachel and Rory. *Out getting our drunk on.*

Bobby laughed, glad she was having a good time. He put his phone back in the center console and headed back to the store to pick up his next delivery. Most of his deliveries took him back to campus because there were always students who didn't go home for the holidays or who came back early to party with their friends over the three-day weekend.

About halfway through his shift he had to stop for gas. He pulled into a small station off University Avenue he liked to use because they were cheap. It was privately owned, without a corporate affiliation, or, if it had one, no visible signage declaring that fact. Bobby groaned when he pulled up to the pump and saw the sign over the card reader that read: *Out of order. Please pay inside.*

Not again.

He got out of the car and went inside the station office that never had more than one person working at a time, handed the attendant a bill, and said, "Twenty on number two."

Without a word, the young man working behind the counter took Bobby's proffered money, rang it up on the register, turned on the pump, and handed Bobby a receipt. He didn't seem to care one way or the other for Bobby's thanks. Before Bobby could turn to leave, the attendant had returned his attention to an iPad propped on the back counter where he had a movie paused.

When Bobby got back to his car he noticed that there were two guys standing outside their vehicle, which they had parked directly behind his. They weren't moving to go inside to pay or making any attempt to do anything at all. It looked as if they were waiting. Waiting for him, but he wasn't sure why—they were unfamiliar to him. Before he could get his hand on the nozzle to start pumping his gas, one of the two guys approached him.

"Your name's Bobby, isn't it?"

"Do I know you?"

"Nope."

"Then how do you know me?"

"Let's just say we know someone in common."

"And who would that be?"

"Can't tell you that, she asked me not to."

"Okay, whatever." Seeming to ignore them, though surreptitiously keeping an eye on them, Bobby reached for the nozzle.

"Our mutual friend, she's not happy with you. She asked us to tell you that."

Not liking the stupid game they were playing and not wanting to play it or play into it, Bobby stayed stoic when he replied, "Fine, message received."

"But see, how do I know that for sure?"

Bobby put the nozzle in his gas tank and put his back against his car. He didn't know what their problem was, but he had a feeling that turning his back on them would be a mistake. Never turn your back on your enemy. And at this moment, they were his enemy.

Both guys stepped in closer to him and the first one was only a few inches from his face. "You ignoring me, freak?"

"Fuck off."

"Oh, I know what you are. And it's fucking disgusting. I say you want to be a man, you should fight like one. What you say? Huh? Can you fight like a man?"

Bobby narrowed his eyes at him, trying to hold his ground. He didn't want this. Just because he was learning how to fight better, didn't mean he wanted to. "I don't need to."

"Oh, you think you're better than me, is that it?" He looked at his buddy. "Did you hear that? He thinks he's better than me. You think you can fucking take me? Here, I'll make it easy for you—you can have the first shot. Right there on the chin." He got in Bobby's face and pointed to his own chin.

Bobby knew when to leave well enough alone. He wasn't afraid of this loser but he did know that two on one he wouldn't stand a chance. He stood up straight and looked the guy in the face and said, "No thanks," and then he finished pumping his gas and went to put the nozzle back in its cradle.

When he turned back around, loser number one grabbed the lapels of Bobby's jacket and threw him up against the side of his car.

"That was the only chance you're going to get." Then he punched Bobby in the stomach and Bobby would have fallen if he wasn't being held up. "Do you know what you did? Do you? She's my sister, man, my sister." With each repetition, he slammed Bobby hard against the car. "She wanted to go to the cops but I told her I'd take care of it because that's what brothers do. I'm going to fucking take care you." With that promise, he hit Bobby in the face. Bobby pushed against him and was able to break away enough that he was standing a few feet away.

He knew he was outnumbered but he wasn't going down without a fight. In the back of his mind he knew he had a split second to flee and it was possible he might have made it, but the odds were against him. After having trained with Dr. Lou for a few weeks, he knew a few kicks and punches that he could use, and he would.

His kick took his first attacker by surprise. Bobby's foot made contact with the man's ribcage and that took him to his knees. Bobby turned to the other one, who was now carrying a wooden baseball bat. Bobby immediately put his hands up in surrender. "No, man, you don't want to do that. I'm done, I'll leave. Just put that down."

The second man looked enraged as he swung the bat wide as if he was going for a grand slam. Bobby put his arms up to try to ward it off as much as he could. He screamed in pain as it made contact and he felt something break in his arm. He couldn't help it—he sank to his knees, cradling his arm to his chest. "Fuck!"

Before the second man could swing his bat again, the first one was on his feet and taking the bat from him. "Give me that, she's my sister." He looked down at Bobby and spit in his face, then said, "You stay away from my sister, you fucking pervert freak."

"I don't even know who she is."

"Oh, you know." Without warning, the man standing over him raised his bat and struck Bobby on his side.

When Bobby fell over, both guys started kicking him. Boots found purchase wherever they could: ribs, face, stomach, groin, chest. Bobby tried to cover his face as best he could, but he only had one arm he could move and when that arm was exposed, it too got struck again. The parting blow was a boot to the face, which cracked Bobby's nose.

The last thing the guy said before he and his buddy got in their car and left was, "That was for Lori, you son of a bitch."

Confused, bloodied, unable to move, Bobby's last thought before passing out into blissful sleep was, *Why?*

Rachel was worried. It was almost two and she hadn't heard from Bobby in over three hours. He had done a good job up until now about contacting her every hour, but with nothing for nearly three hours, she was trying not to look as worried as she felt. While she and Rory were at the bar she kept her phone out on the table the whole time and kept stealing glances at it, hoping Rory wouldn't notice.

"God, you're so rude. You're supposed to be on a date with *me*."

Rachel gave her a wan smile. "Sorry." She turned her phone over so she couldn't see the screen.

"What, no comeback? No witty rejoinder? That's not like you."

"I know. I'm slipping."

"It's okay, I forgive you. Why don't you call him?"

"He might be asleep. I keep telling myself that he probably just got busy at work, then went home and passed out. Nothing to worry about." She put on a brave smile for Rory's benefit but it did nothing to assuage her fear.

"Yeah, that's probably it. Maybe you'll feel better if you just call him."

"I don't want to wake him." Rachel toyed with the straw in her drink.

Gently, Rory said, "Or, you don't want him to not answer and worry you more."

Rachel sighed. "Right. Tell me I'm being stupid."

"I will not. You love him and you're concerned. That's normal."

"I never said I loved him."

Rory said nothing, just smiled and gave Rachel a pointed look over her drink.

"Dammit, Morgan!" In exasperation, Rachel picked up her phone and called Bobby. After five rings his voicemail picked up and she left a message. "Hey, it's me. Just making sure you're all right. Call me when you get this. I don't care what time it is." She disconnected the call and placed her phone upside down on the table. Rory quietly reached over and flipped it back.

"It's okay to be worried. And no, you didn't say you love him, but still."

"Do you make Maggie call you when she goes out of town?"

"All the time. When her plane lands, when she goes to bed, when she leaves. And she will text when she can." Rory laughed. "I *can* live without her but I miss her like crazy and I worry too, though about different things."

"Such as?"

"Normal stuff, like plane crashes, storms, conference hookups." Rory shrugged.

"Conference hookups?"

"Yeah, it's a thing. They're in a hotel, away from home. It happens."

"Morgan, you have nothing to worry about. Maggie loves you and she's not a slut."

"That's true. As you would say, how could she not love me?"

"Right! Who couldn't love us? We're young, hot, and—well, that's all we need."

"Exactly." Rory put her arm around Rachel's shoulders and pulled her closer. Rachel noticed her friend was starting to show the signs of too many longnecks. "Come on, let's dance." Rory stood up and tried to drag Rachel with her to the dance floor.

Laughing, Rachel took hold of Rory's arm and held her ground. "I don't think so. I think it's time to call our ride." Maggie had agreed to be their designated driver but she had declined to stay, giving them their time alone. Rachel had been most grateful.

Rory put both hands on Rachel's shoulders. "You, my friend, need to live a little."

Rachel laughed. "And you, my friend, are drunk. I think it's time to go." She put her arm around Rory's waist and started to propel her toward the door.

"I'm not drunk, I'm an actress."

"You're a drunk actress. You know, for an Irish girl, you can't hold your liquor."

"Sure I can—by the ears!"

"God, you're such an asshole. How you ever found a girl-friend is beyond me."

"Are you forgetting how hot I am?"

"How could I? Come on, let's get some air and I'll call Maggie." They walked out arm in arm, mainly so Rachel could make sure Rory followed. For the next several minutes while she dealt with an inebriated Rory, Rachel almost forgot to worry.

CHAPTER SIXTEEN

Rachel was tossing and turning on the couch. She was tired and the alcohol had definitely made her drowsy, but she knew she wouldn't be able to sleep until she heard from Bobby. She kept imagining all kinds of things that could have happened to him. Then she would chastise herself and tell herself that she was overreacting. She tried to lure herself to sleep with the mantra, *He's fine. He's just asleep. He'll call in the morning. He's fine.*

Just as it was starting to work, a few hours after she and Rory had gotten home from the bar, her phone vibrated on the end table and she quickly reached for it, but was disappointed and curious when it was an unknown number with the same area code as Prairieland. She answered cautiously, "Hello?"

"Rachel?"

Rachel suddenly started to panic and she could feel her heart start to beat faster. Her voice wavered when she answered. "Chris?" Then she asked, almost nonsensically, "How'd you get my number?"

"From Bobby's phone. I'm sorry for waking you."

Her voice came quickly when she asked, "From Bobby's phone? What do you mean, Bobby's phone? Why didn't you just ask him for my number?"

"Because I couldn't," Chris said calmly.

Trying not to cry out, Rachel asked as calmly as she could, "What's wrong?" Something had to be wrong, that's the only reason he would be calling her so early and why Bobby couldn't answer for himself.

"Are you alone?"

"Yes."

"I think you should have someone with you before I tell you."

"Just tell me." She almost yelled, but she recovered and almost whispered, "Just tell me, Chris."

Chris sighed, then began. "First, you should know he's alive. But he was jumped again and beat up pretty badly. He's unconscious and the doctor doesn't know how long that's going to last, or if..." Chris paused and swallowed, then began again. "They did a CT scan and some other things. He's got several broken bones. I'm sorry to be the one to tell you this." There were unmistakable tears in Chris's voice when he stopped talking.

There were tears on Rachel's cheeks that she hastily wiped away and she said, "What hospital?"

Chris told her the hospital and the room number. "You don't have to cut your vacation short. I can keep you updated."

Rachel threw the blanket off and stood up. "No, I'll be there. I have to be there. Thanks for calling." She was about to hang up, when a thought occurred to her. "Is Marissa with you?"

Chris said softly, "Yeah, she's here."

"Good." Rachel hung up and turned and without thinking anything of the time or that there were sleeping people in the house, she called out, "Rory? Oh God, Rory?"

Rory and Maggie came out of their room. Rory was fully dressed and carrying her shoes in one hand and a backpack in the other. "I'm here. I heard." She set her things on the floor and went to Rachel and put her arms around her.

Rachel hugged her and sniffed back tears, but hastily pushed Rory away. "Are you awake enough to drive?"

"Yeah, don't worry. I got this. Go get dressed." Rory lightly touched Rachel on the arm. Then as Rachel found her clothes and went into the bathroom to change, Rory sat on the couch and put on her shoes.

❖

"You're a bad influence on me." Rory gave Rachel a grin and looked at her with a sideways glance, while keeping her eyes on the road.

It meant the world to Rachel that when Rory had heard the panic in her voice, she had gotten dressed and hastily packed her backpack full of clothes, just as she used to do for weekends at Maggie's house. But this was no pleasure trip.

"What do you mean?" Rachel asked quietly, in no mood to play. She kept her hands in her lap and stared out the window.

"I mean the drunk thing. It's been a little over a year since I've been that drunk. You were there."

Rachel smiled. "I remember. You can't blame me for that—you asked me to get you drunk."

"Still, you were there, I'm blaming you."

"Uh-huh."

"Man, your comeback game is weak."

Rachel sighed. "You can't joke me out of this, Morgan, but thank you for trying."

"What are friends for? Do you want to talk about it?"

"I don't know."

"Or we can play really loud music and not talk."

With a small smile, Rachel asked, "Are you always this annoying?"

"It's one of my better qualities."

After a moment, Rachel asked, "Do you think he's going to be okay?"

"What did Chris say his injuries were?"

"A lot of blood loss, broken bones, he's unconscious and they don't know if…" She trailed off and swallowed.

"Well, I'm no expert, but I do know that broken bones heal. I'm sure he'll be fine, given enough time."

"But will he though? I mean, not everything can scab over so easily."

"Yeah, I know. I wish I had something more positive to say right now."

"It's okay." They fell into silence again. Rachel went back to looking out the window but she felt Rory keeping an eye on her.

After a time, Rachel said, with a slight chuckle, "You were right, you know? I love that sweet boy, dammit."

Rory reached over and put her hand on Rachel's knee. "I know, hon, I know." Rachel clasped Rory's hand tightly and they rode that way for the next several miles.

After a mostly quiet five-hour drive, Rory pulled up to the Prairieland Hospital, which was just west of campus. She followed a circuitous route to the visitors' parking lot. The longer it took, the antsier Rachel became. She was about ready to jump out of the car.

"Hold on hon, almost there." Once the car was stopped, Rachel jumped out, leaving the coat she had shed during the long drive behind. Rory grabbed it for her and jogged beside her to the hospital entrance. It took them a couple of minutes to follow the signs leading to the ICU.

When they finally reached their destination, Rachel immediately went up to Chris, who was seated next to a short blond woman, and he stood when she approached.

"Rachel, I'm sorry you had to cut your vacation short, but I'm glad you're here." He nodded to Rory, who returned the gesture, and he gave Rachel a hug.

Before now Rachel had not paid attention to how similar the brothers were in appearance. One look into those same brown eyes and she was almost undone. "No, it's fine. That's not important. I'm just glad you called. How is he? Can I see him?"

An older woman Rachel hadn't noticed before stood up from a chair on the other side of the room. "And who are you?"

"Mom, this is Rachel, she's Bobby's girlfriend. Rachel, our mother."

Very quietly, Rachel replied, "Nice to meet you, Mrs. Lay— uh, I'm just sorry it had to be this way."

The woman drew in an indignant breath and said, "My name is Mrs. James."

"Sorry." Dismissing the woman, Rachel looked at Chris again. "Can I see him?"

"Yes, of cour—"

His mother cut him off. "Only family can see her."

"Or we can give her permission, Mom. Bobby would want Rachel in there."

"Absolutely not! I don't know you from Adam. Why should I give you permission?"

"Ma'am, I love your son very much." Rachel's voice started to break and Rory put her hand on her back. "Why do you think I'm here?"

"Mom, it's okay. I do know Rachel and she's a good person. She really cares for Bobby. Besides, it's not up to you who visits him."

"What are you talking about? That's *my* child in there, of course I have the right to say who gets to see her."

Chris squared off in front of his mother with his hands on his hips and said evenly, "No, Mom, you don't. After Bobby got jumped the last time, he drew up paperwork to make me his health care power of attorney. That means *I* get to make medical decisions for him, not you. And that includes who gets to see him."

"That's ridiculous. Emily is *my* daughter, not yours!" Mrs. James was crying now and wiping furiously at her eyes.

"Your son, Bobby, wanted me in charge because he knew I could keep my cool and do the right thing." Chris softened his voice. "And I know how he feels about Rachel." Chris glanced at Rachel, then back at his mother. "He loves her and she deserves to be by his side and I'm granting permission."

"I know why she picked you. She picked you because you always let your baby sister get away with everything. You spoiled her. You indulged her every whim. And this *Bobby* business is no different. Fine, you both want to cut your mother out of your lives, then I don't need to be here." She turned to the quiet man who had been sitting next to her and who was currently looking uncomfortable yet not willing to intervene, and said, "Come, Howard, we're going home."

"But, Emma, don't you think we should stay? He's not awake yet. I'd like to be here when he wakes up." He stood and tried to take his wife by the arm and guide her to her seat, but she pulled free.

"Don't try and tell me what to do! I'm leaving, come along."

Howard James stood his ground and said, "No, Emma. I'm staying. My youngest son needs me more than you do right now. Go on home if you want. I'll see you there later." With that, he resumed his seat.

Emma James looked from her husband, to her son, and then to Rachel and said, "I don't believe this. I don't believe this." Shaking her head, she walked out, tears on her cheeks. When she left, it seemed as if a sour smell had been let out of the room.

Howard James stood and went to Rachel and held out his hand. "Nice to meet you, dear. I'm sure my son would want to know you're here. Would it be all right if I took you back there?" He held out his arm as if to escort her.

Rachel looked from him to Chris and Rory, both of whom nodded their heads. "Okay, thank you." She put her arm in his and even though it was such an old-fashioned gesture, she was grateful for the support his arm offered.

They left the waiting room arm in arm and Howard led her to the right, down a longish hallway lined with other rooms occupied by the badly injured or sick and dying. All the rooms had large picture windows that looked out into the hallway with an equally large curtain that could be drawn for privacy. Rachel never understood why there was a large window in the first place. Who was that window for? The whole point of visiting was to be in the room, and she could already tell, even though she hadn't seen him yet, that when it wasn't her turn to be in the room, she wouldn't want to sit in the hallway and look in on him lying there, banged up and helpless. She wouldn't be able to bear it. She would need to get away, at least for a little while.

They stopped at the fourth room down on the left and Howard put his hands on Rachel's shoulders. He took a breath, and then he said, "My son is pretty banged up. He has several broken bones, his face is swollen and bruised, and there were internal injuries. He doesn't look good right now but the doctors say he will heal—it'll just take time. He's still unconscious, but that's really a good thing because maybe when he wakes up most of the pain will be gone." His voice broke and he looked down for a moment, then said, "I just wanted you to know what you were walking into."

Rachel couldn't speak to say thank you, so she just nodded. Howard patted her on the shoulder and she took a deep breath.

"Would you like me to wait out here?"

"No, thank you. Could you ask Rory to though?"

"You mean that tall drink of water you walked in with?" He smiled.

Rachel gave him a weak grin in return. "Yeah."

"I will."

Rachel took another breath, then opened the sliding door and stepped inside, closing the door behind her. She stood at the foot of his bed for a moment, taking it in. The beeps and whooshes and whirs of the machinery keeping him alive were the only rhythm and the only sound to be heard in the room. The only sound in Rachel's world. His leg was in traction, an arm was in a cast, his head partially bandaged. The part of his face that was visible was badly bruised and swollen. Black-and-blue was such a wrong way to describe it. It wasn't even accurate. More like black and purple and red. She was frozen at the foot of his bed. She wanted to move forward but she couldn't.

Then some movement on the bed caught her attention. The fingers on his unbroken hand twitched. She knew enough not to hope that it meant he was awake but it still reminded her that he was still in there. That got her moving. She stepped to his side and took his unbandaged fingers in her hand and leaned down and whispered in his ear, "There are better ways to get me to come home early, you big dork." She tried to laugh but it got caught in her throat. "I love you, okay. Did you hear me? I love you and you need to wake up and say it back." She sniffed and wiped her eyes and chuckled to herself. "That's okay, I can wait. I'm not going anywhere. Well, I only have fifteen minutes with you, but I'm not leaving this hospital until you can leave with me. They're going to have to drag me out. While I'm here, I should tell you what my vacation was like. Sweet Boy, let me tell you a story."

She spent the remainder of her time telling him about the last couple of days in Minnesota, until a nurse came in and told her it was time for her to go. She leaned down and whispered, "I have to go now, Sweet Boy, but I'll be back as soon as I can. I love you so much." Then she kissed him on the small space on his cheek that was not discolored and stepped away from the bed slowly, not turning her back on him. Finally, at the last moment, she turned and left.

Rory, who had been patiently standing in the hallway with one boot propped against the wall and her hands behind her back with her head down, came to attention when Rachel stepped out into the hallway. Rachel took two listless steps toward her and

Rory, wordlessly, opened her arms. Rachel went into them, finally letting the tears that she had been holding back fall on
Rory's shoulder.

❖

After Chris and his father had taken their turns sitting with
Bobby, everyone resumed their places in the waiting room, just
hoping for a miracle to happen soon, the same as all the other
waiting, grieving families. Chris sat next to Marissa, who was
holding his hand and patting his arm reassuringly. Rachel was
curled up next to Rory, who had her arm around Rachel's shoulders, and their heads were lolling together.

Rory couldn't help but doze but Rachel had never been more
aware. She stayed cuddled up, however, because she just really
needed to feel Rory's solidness, her nearness. When she heard
Rory start to softly snore she started to feel guilty and realized
she needed to get Rory someplace she could sleep for a while.

She patted Rory on the leg and said, "Hey, Morgan, why
don't you let me drive you to campus? You can sleep in my bed
for a bit."

"No, I'm good," Rory slurred, and shifted some in her seat.

"Uh-huh." Rachel held out her hand. "Are you going to
give me the keys or am I gonna have to go in and get 'em?"

Rory opened her eyes to slits and gave her a tired smile.
"Go for it, Shorty."

"You think I won't? Just because I no longer want to get
into your pants doesn't mean I won't. You're too tired to drive
and the last thing I need is for you to end up in here. Besides, if
I broke you, Maggie would kill me."

"Yeah, you're probably right about that." Rory reached
into her pocket and pulled out Maggie's keys, but before putting them in Rachel's outstretched hand said, "Are you sure you
don't want me to stay?"

Rachel took the reluctantly offered keys and stood up and extended her hand to Rory, who took it and stood too. "I do want you to stay, but you need your sleep more right now."

"So do you."

"I'll get it when I can. I just can't leave yet, you know? You don't have to be here."

"No, I don't, but that's not the point. And you're a bad liar. You're not going to sleep here. Why don't you come back with me and take a nap?"

"Geez, Morgan, stop trying to get me to sleep with you—you're just embarrassing yourself." They exchanged grins. For just a moment, Rachel felt normal again. Not like she had a boyfriend who was lying unconscious and broken just a few feet away. Silently she thanked her friend for that brief gift of normalcy.

"Yeah, yeah. Fine, take me to a bed near you."

Rachel walked over to Chris and said, "I'm going to take Rory to my dorm so she can pass out, but I'll be back."

"You should sleep too."

"I told her the same thing but it didn't work," Rory said, as she leaned back in a stretch.

"Yeah, and I've been saying the same thing to him too, but he won't listen either," Marissa said, giving Chris a smile.

"I think the only one getting a good rest right now is Bobby," Rachel quipped.

Chris gave her an appreciative smile. "Right? The lucky bastard." Chris tried to joke as well but his heart clearly wasn't in it and his words caught at the end. Marissa put her arms around him.

"Um, I'll be back in like fifteen or so. You want me to grab some food on the way back?"

"Actually, that would be great." Chris called out, "Hey, Dad, do you want food? Rachel's going on a food run."

The elder James stirred awake enough to mumble, "Some good coffee and maybe a burger. I don't know."

"That sounds good. Marissa?"

"Sounds perfect."

"Okay." Then Rachel looked around the room, to the other grieving yet hopeful faces, and asked the room at large, "Anyone else want anything while I'm out?"

Everyone looked at her, not speaking up, lost in their own thoughts. What they wanted and needed most she didn't have the power to give them. Finally, a man sitting across the room by himself came to attention. "That sounds good. With fries." One by one the rest of the ICU patients' family members put in their orders. So many that Rachel had to grab a hospital brochure off a nearby table to write them down on.

Once in the car, after buckling herself in, Rory teased, "You never asked if I was hungry."

"That's because I'm not buying you lunch. There's plenty of food in my room. Help yourself."

"Since when do you have real food in your dorm?"

Rachel smiled. "Since I started having a boy over who apparently swallowed a tapeworm. I swear to God, that boy eats like he's never going to see food again. Every two hours seems like, I have to throw food at him."

Rory laughed. "Was he always like that or is it the T, you think?"

"Well, I didn't know him before the T, of course, but I actually asked him that once. He said he's always had a big appetite but the T did increase it."

"I heard it can do that." They fell into silence for a moment but it was obvious that Rory was gearing up to ask another question but wasn't sure how.

In exasperation, Rachel burst out, "What?"

"Well, I also heard it amps up...other appetites as well." Rory snickered.

Rachel instantly blushed. "Okay, yes, I'm dating a horny teenage boy. Happy now?"

Rory couldn't help but laugh. "Not as happy as you are, probably."

"Shut up," Rachel grumbled good-naturedly. Rory said nothing, just continued to giggle to herself.

Once they pulled up at the dorm, Rachel turned to Rory and asked, "Miss it?"

"I miss you but not this place."

Rachel put her hand to her heart and said mockingly, "Aww, got me right here in the feels."

"And you call *me* an asshole."

"You're weren't supposed to remember that—you were drunk."

"Not that drunk. Come on." They got out of the car and walked across the parking lot to the front door of the dorm. The whole time, Rory was looking around at the campus and then the dorm, which hadn't changed at all.

When they got out of the elevator on Rachel's floor, Rory stopped in front of what used to be her room and read the dry-erase board on the door. "Some chick named Julie lives in my room now? What's she like?"

"No idea. Never met her. I may have seen her in the hallway but not sure. She's an undergrad, so our paths don't cross all that much."

"Question—why didn't you move off campus this year?"

Rachel stopped walking halfway down and turned and faced Rory. "Are you implying that I only stayed on campus because you refused to get an apartment with me last year?"

In all seriousness, Rory raised an eyebrow and asked, "Didn't you?"

"Yeah, well, that's not the point. I don't know why I stayed this year. Easier, I guess."

"Hmm."

They were almost to Rachel's door when Lori opened hers. The sight of Rory gave her pause. "Oh, hey, Rory. Rachel, I heard about Bobby. I'm so sorry. Is he okay? Is there anything I can do?"

Rachel instantly tensed and said, "No. Got it covered." Then she went to her door and unlocked it.

Before she and Rory could step inside, Lori called out, "Just let me know if there's anything I can do."

Rachel said nothing.

Once Rory closed the door behind her, she said, "God, she's like an eager puppy."

Rachel sighed. "I know. And she doesn't give a shit about Bobby, but I told you about that already."

"No, she just wants to get on your good side."

"More than that."

"Gathered that." Rory pulled off her leather jacket and put it on the back of Rachel's desk chair, then sat down and took off her boots and placed them under the desk. Rachel stood watching her do it, saying nothing. Rory looked up and caught her looking.

Rachel knew her face was pure grief, that she couldn't hide from Rory.

Rory stood up and went to her and put her hands on Rachel's shoulders. "Honey, what is it?"

Rachel started to shake. "It just…just now, seeing you take your boots off and put them there. He does that. It's not even a strange thing to put your shoes there, it's just that seeing you do it, I just flashed on a memory and…" Rory quickly put her arms around her and Rachel stopped talking.

"It's okay, it's okay."

Rachel didn't cry again because she was choking back the tears, but she held on to Rory as she would a life preserver.

"Everything's going to be okay."

Rachel sniffed, then gave Rory a squeeze before she let go. "Thank you. Sometimes I need that."

"I know. Are you sure you don't want me to go back to the hospital with you?"

"No. You're exhausted. I dragged you out of bed and made you drive me down here with almost no sleep. Just do me a favor and pass out, okay? Please? It'll ease my guilty conscience."

"Nothing to feel guilty about. And you didn't drag me or make me. It's what friends do. Correction, it's what family does. But, just to ease your guilty conscience, I will lie down on your bed and sleep the sleep of the righteous. Just for you! If you need me, call or text or come and get me." Rory kissed Rachel on her forehead, then backed away and started to unbuckle her pants.

"Wouldn't you know, all the times I had hoped that you would be standing in my room getting undressed, and when it finally happens I couldn't care less." She attempted a smile.

"Ouch. I may be engaged, but I still have feelings, you know?" Rory returned the look, then shimmied out of her pants, draped them over the back of the chair, and stood there in her boxers and T-shirt. "I'm about to pull my shirt off so that I can take the bra off. Are you going to keep standing there, perv?"

"Nope, I gotta go. Bobby's in the hospital and suddenly I'm a delivery driver."

"Oh, don't go joyriding in Maggie's car. She'll kill us both."

"What, you mean I can't go drag racing with the boys on Twelfth Street?"

"Don't be sexist. Girls do it too."

"Yeah, yeah. Anyway, I'll take my own car. But speaking of Maggie, you should call her before you go to sleep. And you had better sleep." Rachel pointed her finger at Rory in a menacing fashion.

"Maggie...crap! How could I forget?"

"Blame it on me. I'm sure she'll forgive you. All right, I'm going. Sweet dreams."

CHAPTER SEVENTEEN

It took Rachel nearly an hour to fill all the orders because she decided to treat everyone to burgers from the diner that she and Bobby liked so much. The smells in the car were mouthwatering and she had gotten something for herself, but she wasn't sure how much of it she would be able to eat, even though she knew she should. She called Chris and asked if he could come out and help her carry it all in.

"Thanks for making the food run." Chris took the big box of food and Rachel took the drink caddies.

"No problem. Happy to do it. Anything change while I was gone?"

"One of the families left because their person passed on, sorry to say. But they've been replaced by another family."

"That's sad. What about Bobby?"

"The same. Still unconscious but everything's reading normal otherwise."

"Good." Rachel was quickly learning that what passed for normal in the ICU meant breathing on one's own, heart rate and blood pressure steady. She was now living in a world where stable was the best one could hope for.

"His doctor is making his rounds now, so we should know more soon."

"Okay, good." Rachel realized that she had never spoken to Chris more than she had in the last few hours. The few times he had been at the house when she had come by, they had done nothing more than trade quips, while he and Bobby tossed good-natured insults back and forth. He was a fun guy to be around but she didn't know him very well. It really sucked, she thought, that it took tragic events for people to become better acquainted.

Chris and Rachel distributed the food and drinks, giving the new family the order that had been purchased for the one who had left. Everyone was into their food when a nurse came to the waiting room and called out, "Mr. James, the doctor is with your brother right now. You said you wanted to speak with him."

Chris put down his food and stood immediately. "Yes, yes. Coming. Rachel, you want to come with me?"

Somewhat startled, Rachel said, "What? Oh yes." She got up and followed him down the hall to Bobby's room where the doctor was updating Bobby's chart. He turned when Chris and Rachel walked in.

The doctor explained Bobby's injuries in more detail and mentioned that the biggest concern was whether or not Bobby had a concussion or an even worse brain injury. Sadly, it was something that they just had to wait and see about. In the mean-time, he was unconscious and all they could do was monitor him and hope for the best.

Once the doctor was out of the room, Rachel said, "Wait and see? Wait and see?" Rachel's voice became shriller with the repetition of the question, and Chris put his arm around her and she tried to get control of herself. "Prick."

Rachel stepped away from Chris and ran her fingers through her hair. For the first time, she focused on the reason they were there. She walked over to the bed and took Bobby's hand and ca-ressed his face, then leaned down and whispered in his ear, "Wake up, Sweet Boy, it's time to get up. Don't worry, everything's going to be okay. I'm right here. I love you. I love you so much." The tears took over her voice and she couldn't speak anymore. She put her head down on the bed next to his uninjured hand

and whispered, "Don't leave me, not yet. Please." She kissed his fingers one by one, then held his hand to her cheek. As she did so, his fingers twitched but there was no other movement.

Rachel sniffed and wiped her eyes. "I know what you want. You want me to sing for you, don't you, Sweet Boy? Okay. Um… for some reason, only one song is coming to mind right now." Though she had never considered herself a religious person, her parents had raised her in a Protestant home and her mother was a fan of contemporary Christian music. She began to softly sing a song from her childhood that had always touched her, "The Warrior is a Child."

When the song was over she whispered, "You *are* amazing. You are." She looked up and realized that Chris had walked out of the room, maybe to give them privacy. Being sweet must run in the family.

She stayed by Bobby's side until a nurse found her there several minutes later and told her that her time was up. She kissed him on the cheek again, sighed, and said, "I have to go for now, but you know I'll be back." As she left the room she almost wished she hadn't sent Rory away, but she knew Rory needed her sleep. She knew she did too, but she felt jazzed up, as if on caffeine, though it was probably just an adrenaline rush. She would crash when her body couldn't take any more, but she hoped it wouldn't be anytime soon.

❖

By the afternoon, everyone was doing the waiting game. Marissa had had to leave for work and Bobby and Chris's father had reluctantly, and only at Chris's urging, gone home to rest. So Chris and Rachel were there alone, making small talk or occasionally sleeping in shifts, if you could call what Rachel did sleeping. They took their turns by Bobby's bedside each hour.

At one point, Rachel turned to Chris and said, "We're not engaged, you know?"

"I know. You know why I told the medical team that though, right?"

"I do. Thank you for defending me to your mother too, by the way. I know his history with her."

"Yeah, figured you did. I'm glad you're here—he needs you." Chris took her hand and squeezed it.

"He needs you too. I know you're the biggest advocate he has in the family."

"Yeah. Dad surprised me though. For years he's kept his mouth shut whenever Mom would talk against Bobby, and we just figured he felt the same way she did."

"What's her problem, anyway? I mean, hasn't it sunk in that she's going to lose him? I mean, by him cutting her out of his life, not by…" She trailed off, stricken by what she'd said.

"It's all right, I knew what you meant. And to answer your question"—Chris's voice was vehement and bitter now—"her *God* is what's getting in the way of her seeing that her child has been there the whole time. He's just not the child she always thought he was."

"Hell, I'm definitely not the sweet little girl my parents thought they were getting either, but they accept me, even when I'm getting on their last nerve. You don't know this about me, but I have a great knack for getting on people's nerves."

Chris threw back his head and laughed.

"Maybe he doesn't know that about you, but I do," Rory said.

Rachel turned at the sound of her voice. "Rory, what are you doing back here?" Rachel stood and threw her arms around her friend. Despite her words, she was grateful to see her there. Rory hugged her back, then nodded to Chris when Rachel let go.

"I just needed a few hours of sleep, I'm all good now." Rory shrugged out of her jacket and took a seat.

Rachel snickered. "Are you still hungover?"

"I surpassed hungover hours ago, thank you very much. I would have been here sooner but I had to find food."

"I told you there was food in my room."

"Yeah, microwavable crap. Is that what you feed him? Poor boy."

"Not all of us have a kitchen at our disposal."

"Not all of us can be a ninja in that kitchen either." Rory grinned.

Rachel curled her lip at her. "Yeah, well, at least I still have the pretty thing." Rory said nothing, just raised an eyebrow. "Okay, bad example. There must be *something* I have that you don't have."

"Well, I don't have a boyfriend, there's that."

"Yeah," Rachel said wistfully. She realized that both Chris and Rory were smiling at her. Rory took her hand again and Rachel held tightly to it. "No, but you have a Maggie and that's almost as good."

"Definitely. And before you ask, I *did* call her. I don't remember hanging up though."

"Mr. James?" The nurse interrupted their reunion. Everyone in the waiting room besides Chris, Rachel, and Rory looked away when she called Chris's name.

Chris stood up and Rachel and Rory followed. "Is he awake?"

"Not fully but he is coming to. I figured you'd want to be there."

Chris put his hand at Rachel's waist. "Can his fiancée come as well?" If Rory was surprised at the word fiancée, she kept quiet.

The nurse smiled at Rachel. "Of course."

Rachel turned to Rory. "Can you…"

"Wait where I did before?" Rachel nodded. "Yes."

The walk to Bobby's room was different this time. There was not as much a sense of dread as there had been the other times they had taken that path. Rory held Rachel's hand as they made the short walk down and Chris stopped midstride. "I need to call Dad. You go ahead—I'll be in in a minute." He pulled out his phone and began to pace a path in the hallway while he waited for his father to answer his phone.

Rory squeezed Rachel's hand, then leaned down and gave her a kiss on the cheek. "This is good. He's going to be okay."

"I know." Rachel gave her a brave smile. She took a breath again, though she wasn't sure why because she knew this time was going to be different. Granted, he was still going to look the same and the machines were still going to be there, but this time he would know she was there. He could hear her say she loved him. As she expelled her breath, she slid open the door and went inside.

What she saw when she walked in was the best thing she could have hoped for. Bobby's eyes were open and he looked at her and he knew her. She could tell by the way his eyes crinkled and started to form tears. He tried to lift his unbroken arm but didn't seem to have the energy.

She went to him and took his hand in hers. "Hi. Welcome back."

He made a gargling noise around the breathing tube in his throat and became frustrated when he realized he couldn't talk.

"It's okay, don't worry about it. It'll be out soon enough. Well, easy for me to say, right? I don't have a large tube down *my* throat. All things in time. What matters is that you're awake."

He gripped her hand tightly and the tears that looked imminent when he first saw her started to fall, and he turned his head away from her.

"Stop that! Don't be afraid to cry, you have every reason to cry. We all do because we love you."

He turned his head sharply in her direction and his eyes widened.

"That's right, you heard me. I love you and not because of this. I mean, I've loved you for a while. I just hadn't given myself a chance to admit it. So there, now you know." She brushed the tears off his cheeks and leaned down and kissed him there.

He gripped her hand hard but she didn't mind. When she stood back up he was nodding.

"Yes what, Sweet Boy, yes what?" She looked him in the eye for a moment and then she understood. "You love me too?" she asked softly.

He nodded again.

"I know. I think I've known that for a while too."

Before she could say any more, Chris walked in accompanied by the doctor and a nurse.

"So, I hear you're coming around, Mr. Layton. We're just going to check a few things for you, then see if we can get that annoying tube out of your throat. Before we do that, I just want to tell you that you're going to probably be a little hoarse for a while, but don't worry, it's not permanent. You may experience a gagging sensation at first, which is perfectly normal. The important thing is not to panic. If you panic, it won't be a pleasant experience. But I see your fiancée's here, so allow her to keep you calm."

As the doctor consulted the machines attached to Bobby, Bobby looked at Rachel, clearly confused.

Rachel just said, "Shh, not now."

Chris came to stand next to Rachel. "Hey, buddy. It's been a day." Bobby nodded then glanced at the doctor.

"Okay, it looks like all your numbers are normal and now we can take out the tube. Are you ready?"

Bobby nodded and Chris stood to the side so the nurse could take his place, but Bobby held firm to Rachel's hand and she stayed where she was. The removal of the tube and accompanying apparatus only took a matter of seconds, and it made Bobby gag and cough. The nurse was there with a cup of water and she had to remind him not to gulp it down. Even so, some water spilled out of his mouth because he had taken too much.

He lay back against his pillows and tried to speak but the words wouldn't come. You could tell how much it hurt him to talk by the strain on his face.

The doctor said, "I'm sorry to say that it might be a couple of days before you can speak. And when you do, you may have to take care so as not to strain your throat. But don't worry, it'll pass. It'll just be like having a scratchy throat that eventually goes away. Everything looks good. Now you just have to get on the road to full recovery." He smiled, and then he and the nurse left.

Chris moved back to the spot he'd vacated. "Dad's on the way. He said if you fall back asleep before he gets here, that's okay, he'll wait for you."

Bobby tried to whisper but it was obvious it pained him, so he mouthed one word instead.

"Mom?" Chris asked. Bobby nodded.

Chris looked at Rachel for a second and then said, "She went home this morning. She'll be back."

Bobby shook his head.

"You don't know that," Rachel said.

Bobby just shook his head again.

Rachel leaned down and whispered in Bobby's ear, "I meant what I said. I love you and I need you to recover quickly so I can take you home." She kissed his lips very gently and was relieved when he kissed her back. Rachel heard the door slide open and turned to see a nurse standing there and knew she and Chris had to go. "We have to go now, baby, but we're just down the hall and we're not going anywhere. I'll be back later."

Now that he was awake, it was hard to leave him there. Before there had been no emotion on his face, but now there were several, and she knew them all, and she wanted to just crawl into bed with him and curl up with him and sing him to sleep.

And something else was starting to take hold finally now that she knew he was better: anger. Someone did this to him for the sole purpose of hurting him. She had no idea who or why, but she hated *them* with almost as much intensity as she loved him.

When she got back out to the hallway, Rory was standing there with a questioning look, waiting for her cue as to what Rachel needed from her. There were no tears this time when Rachel put her arms around her friend, despite the anger welling up; she was still happy and so very grateful.

"He's awake and off the breathing tube. He's going to be okay, Morgan. He's going to be okay."

Rory hugged her tight and said, "I knew he would be. I always knew he would be."

By evening, Chris decided to go home and sleep, especially after Marissa threatened him, with what he wouldn't say. Miraculously, Rory had convinced Rachel to do the same, but only with the explicit promise of getting up with the sun to come back in the morning.

Rachel went in to say good night to Bobby.

He kept trying to speak.

"Honey, please stop. You're just going to hurt yourself. As much as I would love to hear your voice right now." She smiled at him and he started to mouth something. "What? I'm sorry, I can't make that one out."

He was growing more frustrated and balled his fist on the mattress, but Rachel took his hand and unclenched it. "Baby's it's okay."

He fumbled with her hand until it lay palm open, and intrigued, she watched as he began to write letters there with his index finger one at a time, pausing until she said each letter out loud.

"Lori? What about her?"

He raised his arm and gestured to his broken body.

Understanding was starting to dawn. "She did this?" Rachel asked, incredulous.

Bobby shook his head and spelled in her hand again.

"Bro? Do you mean *brother*?" He vigorously nodded. "You mean Lori's brother beat you up?"

He nodded again and then wrote one more thing.

"Two? Two what, two brothers?"

Bobby shrugged.

"So it was Lori's brother and at least one more person?" He nodded. "That fucking bitch. What in the bloody hell?" Quickly getting her anger under control, Rachel leaned down and kissed him on the lips, then said, "I have to go for now. I promise, I'm going to get some sleep tonight, but first I'm going to kick that crazy bitch's ass."

Bobby gripped her arm tightly and shook his head.

"Oh, don't worry, I won't get hurt or arrested, but she will. I haven't decided which yet. I love you, Sweet Boy, and I'll see you in the morning. Don't worry." She kissed him again, gently disengaging herself from his grip.

When she got back out into the hallway, she grabbed the strap on the bottom of Rory's leather jacket and pulled her along, as if the strap was a leash, and said, "Come on, Morgan, we have to go kick someone's ass."

Amused, Rory allowed herself to be pulled. She asked, "And who would that be?"

"You'll see."

"Am I going to need bail money?"

"Probably."

"Sweet."

CHAPTER EIGHTEEN

Rachel brought Rory up to speed on the drive to the dorm. As they pulled into the parking lot, Rory asked, "So, what are you going to do?"

"I don't know."

"Just to be clear, am I here to help you commit a felony or to stop you?"

"I don't know yet. You think I've had time to plan?" Rachel parked at an angle two spots from the door of the building, the best parking spot she'd ever gotten.

Rory put a hand on Rachel's arm before she could run out of the car. "Rachel, you know I've got your back no matter what, but I want you to seriously stop and think a minute before you go charging in there. Do you really think she's going to admit to it? Would it really be worth it to hit her?"

Rachel thought it over. Then she said, "Tell me something, Morgan, what if it was Maggie? What would you do?"

Rory took a moment before she responded, and then she said quietly, "I would do what I had to do."

"Then you know how I feel. Come on."

As they walked down the hallway to Lori's door, Rachel couldn't help but feel as if she was in an old-time Western, about to have a duel. The actor in her really wished she was wearing a duster, a Stetson, and a six-shooter. Spurs would have come in handy too, she thought.

When she reached Lori's door, she almost surprised herself by knocking calmly. Before she knocked she had the thought that Lori might not be home, but she heard movement and suddenly Lori was standing in front of her, obviously surprised to see them.

"Hi." She looked from Rachel to Rory and back again. "Is something wrong? Is it Bobby? Oh my God, is he okay?" She put her hand over her mouth and looked horrified at the possibilities.

Rory snorted but otherwise kept quiet.

"Oh no, he's fine. As a matter of fact, he woke up and he's talking." A lot of emotions played out on Lori's face at Rachel's half-truth. "I think you know what I'm about to say."

"No, I…really don't."

"Yeah, you do. And I gotta tell you, I don't know what to do right now. I just can't believe…I just don't know what to think. I mean, why? Can you at least tell me that?"

"Why, what?"

"Don't, just don't. I'm trying really hard not to drop-kick your skinny ass down this hallway." Rory put her hand on Rachel's arm but didn't say anything. Rachel immediately calmed down. "Look, you know as well as I do what Bobby said when he woke up. Why else would I even be here? I left the bedside of the man I love to come knock on your door. Why do you think I did that? Huh?"

Lori was starting to get nervous. She looked to Rory for help but Rory just shrugged as if to say, *You're on your own.* A look crossed Lori's face and a resolve settled over her. "You don't know?"

"I really don't."

Lori crossed her arms over her chest and looked at Rachel defiantly but said nothing.

Rory said, "Oh my God, I get it."

"Well, will you tell me?" Rachel asked.

"In her warped mind, she thinks that if she got Bobby out of the picture, then she could get you back. That's it, isn't it?"

"Really? You think I would come running back to you in my time of grief?"

Lori snarled. "I should have known you'd call her." She nodded to Rory. "Does Bobby know that she's the one you really love?"

Rory sneered and tilted her head to Rachel. "You want me to do something with this garbage?"

"Nope, I'm done. I just wanted to hear her say it. I just wanted to hear her say she got Bobby beat up."

"Yeah, well, he lived, so no harm, no foul, right?"

"You do know you've committed a felony, right?" Rory asked, incredulous.

"You're joking. I never touched him."

"But you hired your brother to do it, that's a felony," Rachel said.

"Whoa, whoa, whoa, I didn't pay him—I just told him I didn't like him. What he did, he did on his own. What, you going to call the cops or something? Good luck with that. I didn't do anything."

"No, it's not for me to do, that's Bobby's choice."

"Then why are you here?"

"Like I said, I just wanted to hear what you would say. I'm done." She narrowed her eyes at Lori, then started to walk away, but stopped and turned back around. "Oh, and for the record, even if there was no Bobby, I would never want to get back with you. You're a crazy, messed up little bitch and I never really liked you. You were just easy and convenient." Rachel smirked at her.

Lori's eyes blazed. "You fucking bitch, I'll kill you!" She charged Rachel and tried to put her hands around her neck, but Rachel was quick and was able to get her arms up in a defensive move she had learned in her kung fu lessons. The move enabled her to quickly stop Lori's hands and bat them away, and then Rachel grabbed one wrist, bent it back, and twisted Lori's arm behind her back and pushed her against the wall.

Lori cried out.

"Oh, stop whining," Rachel said. "It's not like I hit you. That would have really hurt."

"You're hurting me now."

"Really? Really?" With each repetition, Rachel applied more pressure to Lori's wrist. "You nearly killed him! Do you even understand that? You nearly fucking killed him and you're whining because I'm bending your wrist. How fucking dare you?"

Rory leaned in to Rachel and said with evident glee, "Um, as much as I'm enjoying this, you can't keep her against the wall like this forever. And you've drawn a crowd."

Rachel looked at Rory and then at the onlookers and calmly said, "You're right, my arms will get tired."

Rory cocked her head in the direction of Rachel's room. "Come on, let's go to your room and I'll buy pizza."

"Pizza sounds good." Rachel gave one final twist to Lori's wrist then let her go.

"You fucking assaulted me, you bitch!"

"Actually, you attacked her," Rory noted, "and I don't think I'm the only one who saw that."

Molly shouted her agreement from the crowd. Several others in the group joined her.

"Go to hell." Lori went back into her room and slammed her door.

The crowd cheered and some immediately started asking questions, but Rory held up one hand, while she put her other arm around Rachel's waist and steered her toward Rachel's room.

"All right, that's enough. She's had a really long day. Come on."

Rachel said nothing as Rory led her to her room and closed and locked the door behind them.

Rory smiled at her. "You provoked Lori on purpose, didn't you?"

"You think I'm stupid? I'm not going to start a fight. But I will damn sure finish one."

Rory laughed. "How'd it feel?"

"Good. Not half as good as punching her would have, but still good."

"Good. Way to go, you really are a ninja." Rory lifted her hand for a high five and Rachel slapped it.

"I owe it all to my *sifu*." Rachel bowed to Rory as she would to her trainer.

Amused, Rory bowed back. "You're not paying that woman nearly enough."

"Tell me about it."

❖

On Sunday Bobby was able to talk more clearly, and at Chris's insistence, filed a police report and formal charges against Lori, her brother, and the unknown friend, who were all arrested later in the day. Rachel almost regretted not being in the dorm when it happened, but she listened to Rory's advice that it was best to stay away until later.

Later that day, Rory finally headed home. She protested, but Rachel ordered her to leave. Rachel knew she'd feel guilty if she kept Rory away from home for too long.

"Just remember, call me anytime for anything."

"I know and I will. I just...I want to say..."

"I know. You would do the same for me."

"In a heartbeat. I just hope to God I never have to." They hugged and Rachel hid her face in Rory's jacket in the hope that she wouldn't see her tears. Rory rubbed Rachel's back and kissed her cheek. When they parted, Rachel sniffed and said, "I love you, asshole."

Chuckling, Rory said, "I love you too."

"No, jerk, you did it wrong. It doesn't count unless you insult me."

Rory laughed. "Oh, sorry. I love you too, douche."

"Aww, thank you. Now go home and give that woman waiting for you a big kiss from me."

"I will. And keep me updated on every little thing."

"Okay, the next time he takes a piss I'll let you know."

"Okay, maybe not every little thing."

After Rory left, Rachel stayed in the hospital until Bobby had been settled in a new room on the surgical floor. His voice wasn't a hundred percent yet, but he could manage a clear whisper. He clasped Rachel's hand tightly. "I love you. I should have said it sooner."

"Sooner, later, doesn't matter. The point is you said it and I'm going to hold you to it." They shared a smile and she brought his fingers up for a kiss.

"Good, do that."

"Oh, trust me, you're not getting out of it now. Locked in. Face it, you're in love with a *lesbian*."

Bobby feigned a look of horror. "Well, you're in love with a *dude*."

"Hmm…maybe I didn't think this through." She winked at him, then leaned over and kissed his lips. She was delicate and knew she couldn't linger because of his broken nose, but she really wanted to.

It was Bobby, however, who whined in protest when she pulled away. "I miss you. I mean, I miss sleeping with you. I know you would stay if I asked, but I want you to get a good night's sleep. I know I will, with all the drugs I'm currently on."

"Yeah, I don't have the same help. But I promise, I'll go home and sleep." Feeling devilish, she pretended to look contrite. "I have to confess something. I slept with Rory last night." It was hard to suppress a grin and after a couple of failed attempts, she stopped trying.

Bobby didn't look upset in the slightest. "Oh, was it good for you?"

"Not nearly as awesome as I always thought it'd be. She generates way more body heat than you do and she's freakishly tall, so it was like sleeping next to a tree, a very warm tree."

"Liar." Bobby was still grinning. "You're just trying to protect my ego. Besides, you know I trust you."

"Well, that just takes the fun out of it." She sighed. "But I know. Besides, I was little more than a blond body pillow for her anyway."

What she would never tell him was that in the middle of the night, after Rory had rolled over and gone to sleep, the stress and fear of the last twenty-four hours had finally gotten to her. She had lain as far in the corner as she could and let the tears quietly come. A few minutes later, Rory shifted and was suddenly snuggled up behind her and had put her arm around Rachel, enveloping her in a hug. She had taken Rachel's hands and whispered, "I know, hon, I know. It's okay. He's going to be okay now. It's okay, I got you." Rachel scooted closer and Rory held her tighter. Rachel knew that she had never loved her best friend more.

After she went back to her dorm after saying good night to Bobby, she ignored all attempts from her neighbors to get her attention. As much as she wanted to hear about the arrest, at the same time, she just didn't care. When she got to her room, she fell across the bed with a sigh, jacket and shoes still on. She rolled over onto her side, cradling her pillow in her arms, and stared at the wall.

She wasn't sure what she felt like doing: sleeping, screaming for joy, running away, all of the above. She wasn't aware of dozing until a couple hours later when her phone nearly made her jump by buzzing in her pocket. It was Rory. She was just calling to let her know she had arrived safe and to tell her that Maggie sent her regards.

Rachel briefly wondered what the fuck that even meant, when someone sent their regards. Was that prayers for the non-religious? "Stop it, you're being mean," she chastised herself. The truth was, she liked Maggie and Maggie's kindness meant a lot to her.

The next morning, she awoke semidressed, having shed all the lower half of her clothing except her underwear and having thrown off her bra and sweater in favor of a T-shirt she had found on the floor. She'd pulled it on after smelling the cologne. She knew it was Bobby's and that had made her smile as she had fallen asleep. Now she headed to the shower.

Once refreshed, she remembered that her classes started back up today after the Thanksgiving holiday and wasn't sure if she had the energy to sit through class. She was torn. She had a feeling Bobby would tell her to go to class even if he did want her to stay with him. She also had training with Dr. Silver later in the day.

She suddenly realized she wanted to see that wise, sensible woman again.

Chapter Nineteen

The door was open when she got to Dr. Silver's office a few minutes later. She walked in without knocking and wordlessly set a cup of coffee on the professor's desk before taking a seat and removing the lid of her own cup to blow on it.

"Well, good morning, Rachel. What have I done to deserve free coffee today?"

"For starters, you taught me kung fu."

"Correction, I am *teaching* you kung fu. You're not done yet."

"Good point. But I just wanted to tell you that I've already had to put some of it to use."

"Oh? Sounds like you had an interesting Thanksgiving."

"I wish I hadn't."

"What do you mean?"

Rachel sighed and stretched her legs out in front of her. "Well, it started out great. I went to visit my friend Rory and her fiancée in Minnesota."

"Well, that sounds good," Lou said cautiously.

"Oh, seeing Rory was awesome. But it was cut short." Rachel sighed and looked away. Dr. Silver gave her a concerned look but kept quiet. Finally, Rachel said, "Bobby's brother called to tell me that Bobby got jumped."

"Oh my God! Is he okay?" Lou sat up in her chair. Her concern was obvious and it appeared that she was ready to leap into action.

Rachel appreciated Lou's response. It was good to know Lou cared that much for him. It made her feel that she had done the right thing in coming here.

"Getting there. But it was really scary for a while. Thank God for Rory." Rachel proceeded to tell an increasingly concerned Dr. Silver all that had transpired, concluding with the arrests.

Still looking rather upset, Dr. Silver asked, "Do you think his family would allow me to see him?"

"Oh, he's out of the ICU so anyone can visit now. I'm actually going there when I leave here. Want to go together?"

Rachel hoped she didn't sound as needy as she felt, but she really wanted someone with her. She felt like the weakest person in the world lately, considering she always seemed to collapse into tears or emotional exhaustion every time she saw Bobby.

Dr. Silver eyed Rachel for a moment. She had a way of looking right through her that made her feel exposed. *Thank God I don't have sexual thoughts about her*, Rachel thought. *She'd probably read me like a book.* A smutty book at that.

Finally, Lou said, "Yes, I would. Oh, and Rachel?"

"Yeah?"

"You're a strong person, stronger than you realize, and from the sound of it, you have held up better than could be expected."

Softly, Rachel said, "Then why do I feel like the weakest link?"

Lou leaned forward and reached for Rachel's hand. "Rachel, I know I don't know all the details and I can't know exactly how you feel but just know this: Being strong doesn't mean no emotion. It doesn't mean you don't cry. It doesn't mean you don't rage. Being strong means feeling all of it, taking it all in, and then going back. Strength is not the suppression of emotion—it's the *endurance* of emotion. It's the ability to get back up and do it all over again because you have to. Does that make sense?"

Wordlessly, Rachel nodded.

Dr. Silver smiled. "You know, even warriors cry when the battle is over."

"Trust me, I've done plenty of that."

"Good." She squeezed Rachel's hand and Rachel gave her a grateful smile, and then Lou stood up. "Come on. Let's go see that sweet boy of yours." Lou grabbed her jacket off the back of her chair and Rachel stood with her.

"Would this be a good time to tell you I may not make it to class today?"

"We'll see about that, Ms. Cole, we'll see about that." With her ever-present mysterious grin, Lou opened her office door and gestured Rachel out, then followed behind her.

When Rachel and Lou arrived, Chris met them in the hallway outside Bobby's door and gave Rachel a hug. "Good morning. Everything's good so far. The CT showed no further bleeding and he's talking. Oh, and our mother is here. She's with him now. So far, nothing's exploded." Then he noticed Lou. "I'm sorry, I'm being rude. I'm Chris, Bobby's brother." He held out his hand.

Shaking it, Lou said, "No worries. I'm Lou Silver, one of Rachel's professors, and I'm teaching both of them kung fu."

"That's you?" Lou nodded. "Thank you. He told me that he was able to get some shots in. The kicks he did brought one of them to his knees. It may have slowed him down some. Bobby said he knows he hurt him. So thank you for what you're doing. He definitely needs to learn some survival skills."

"It's my pleasure to teach them. I just wish I'd had time to teach him more before he needed to use it. I'm glad he's doing better. Would it be all right if I saw him?"

"Oh, yeah, yeah. You're in line after Rachel. Let me go see if I can get my mom moving."

"I can wait," Rachel said. "If it's going well, let them be. That is, unless you think he needs a break from her."

"Let me go check." Chris disappeared into Bobby's room and Rachel and Lou exchanged small smiles but said nothing.

Chris came back a couple of minutes later with his mother, who went up to Rachel. When she got closer, Rachel saw the redness in her eyes from crying.

"Rachel." Rachel nodded. "My dau—my *son* told me a lot about you. He said he loves you." Rachel nodded again. "See what you can do about getting him to my house for Sunday dinner when he gets out of the hospital, would you?"

"Yes, ma'am, I'll do my best."

"Good." She exhaled, then looked at Chris. "Walk me out." She nodded to Rachel and Lou, even though she didn't take the time to learn who Lou was. Chris just nodded to both of them then led his mother out.

Rachel grabbed Lou's hand. "Come on, you're going in with me."

"Don't you want to be alone?"

"I have had plenty of alone time with him and I will have more. Thought you might need the moral support." Rachel's look faltered and it made Lou smile. "In all seriousness though, he is a sight to see and it is off-putting at first. Lots of broken bones and his face is a mess."

"I can take it if you can."

"I've been taking it all weekend. Okay, let's go." Rachel pushed open the door and almost forgot Lou as soon as she saw Bobby. He was sitting up more and his smile was bigger.

"Rachel."

That was the best part of all—he said her name.

"Hey, Dr. Lou." He gave them both a big smile.

"Hi, Bobby," Lou said.

"There's that voice I've missed so much." Rachel went to him and kissed him on the lips, not caring that Lou was there.

"Yeah, it came back this morning."

"I saw your mother. Everything okay?"

"Yeah, it's good. She called me her son." His face lit up at the words.

"I know, she said it to me too. Honey, I'm so glad."

"Me too. Oh, Doc, I wanted to thank you. I was able to use some of the stuff you taught me." Despite the bruises and bandages on his face, the smile he wore made him look like a young boy.

"You're welcome. I'm glad. I hope you broke something on him. When you get out of here, I'll teach you more defensive moves."

"Yes! Can use more of those."

"Rachel, I'm going to step out into the hall. Do you want me to wait for you?"

"Would you?"

"Of course. Bobby, we need you on your feet as soon as possible. So do whatever the doctors tell you and let this woman take care of you too." Lou rubbed Rachel's shoulder and gave Bobby a smile.

"I promise to listen to all my doctors, Dr. Silver." He grinned. Lou laughed. Rachel lightly smacked him on the shoulder. "Ow, what was that for?"

"Stop flirting." She grinned at him and he turned beet red.

"As I said, listen to her." Dr. Lou waved as she left them alone.

❖

When Rachel came out into the hallway Lou was standing against the wall with her arms crossed against her chest. She came forward at Rachel's approach. "You okay?"

"Yeah. He's doing better, and now we just have to wait for his body to heal, but the point is, he will." Rachel attempted a smile and it almost made it to her face.

"Good. He's a strong boy and I know he's determined. Now my concern is you." Lou leveled her gaze at Rachel and Rachel started to squirm.

"What? I'm fine." Rachel shifted her feet but held Lou's gaze, which instantly made the hospital hallway disappear for Rachel. She felt like they were in session again and that whatever Lou said next would require a bow from her in response.

"No, you're not fine." Her tone, though gentle and kind, brokered no argument. "If you can't rest your mind enough to come to class today, that's understandable. But you *will* come to work out with me today. You can leave him for a couple of hours—it will do you good."

"But—"

"No. You will be there. On time and ready to work. Trust me." During her declaration, Lou had put her arms behind her back and Rachel had instinctually followed her example. Instead of bowing, which Rachel figured would have been inappropriate to their location, Lou nodded to Rachel and Rachel, understanding the gesture, did the same.

Quietly, she said, "Yes, Sifu. I'll be there."

"Good. You stay, I'll walk back. I'll see you this afternoon." Lou walked away and Rachel exhaled.

Once Lou was out of earshot, Rachel muttered, "Bobby's right. That woman's intense."

Rachel walked into their training space on time. Lou was right; Bobby had told her he was okay about her going, more than okay. He was kind of jealous, he said, since he wished he could have gone too. With Bobby's declaration of, "Kick some ass for me too," in her ears, Rachel took her place on the mat and bowed to Lou and tried to clear her head.

Lou was wearing headgear and a pair of strange gloves that were open on the palm. On the floor next to her was another pair of gloves, a mouth guard, and the same headgear. She handed them to Rachel.

"After your warm-up, put these on. Oh, and when you get home tonight, make sure you boil that"—she indicated the mouth guard—"and fit it to your mouth. You don't want it to be loose."

"Okay, but why are we sparring today?"

Lou raised an eyebrow and Rachel immediately ducked her head.

"I mean, yes, Sifu." She had never played sports in school, except for whatever sociopathic nonsense she had had to endure in PE class, so she had never had occasion to wear a helmet. After her warm-up, she did as instructed and strapped it on, along with the gloves, which she knew were sparring gloves. They had never sparred before and she wondered why now. She thought it was too soon in her training, though she trusted Lou knew what she was doing.

"Okay, today, as you may have surmised, we are going to spar a little. I have taught you a set of moves, and now I want you to use them. Use the punches, use the kicks. Do you remember them?"

"Yes, Sifu."

"Do not hesitate to strike me. Rest assured I can take care of myself. If you hesitate, make no mistake, I will seize the opportunity. You remember the contact rules?"

"Yes. Stay away from the back of your head, your neck, throat, and back, as well as your joints and groin. Using my knees or head-butting is also not cool."

Rachel thought she caught Lou smiling at her colloquialism before resuming her serious expression.

"And if you best me and I take a knee or say *tap out*, how do you respond?"

"Wow, best you, I don't think that's going to happen. But if I were to pull off that miracle, I back off."

"Okay. Good."

Lou bowed to Rachel and Rachel bowed in return. Then Lou stepped away to take a fighting stance, put in her mouth guard, and gestured for Rachel to do the same.

"Begin!"

They danced around each other for a while, both with their hands up in a defensive position. Rachel shut out the room and the noises and worries in her head and focused on watching Lou. She watched how her body moved and she looked for vulnerabilities. At first, she couldn't see any. Lou was too good at protecting herself and Rachel wasn't sure how she was going to approach an attack on this woman who had been studying kung fu long enough to earn a black belt.

Then she noticed something. Lou had a tendency to drop her right hand just a bit and expose her chin. It was only for a small fraction of time but Rachel thought that if she was quick enough, she could get a hit in.

She waited for the right moment. She concentrated on the spot she was going to strike and shut out the voice reminding her that she was about to punch her teacher in the face and went for it without hesitation.

The look on Lou's face at the blow was awesome.

"Ha!" Rachel cheered in triumph.

Lou took the opportunity afforded by Rachel's victorious exclamation and struck her in the side. They went on this way for several minutes, Rachel constantly surprising herself each time she got a hit in.

There would be no winner to declare, Rachel suspected, not because she was holding her own, but because Lou was going easy on her. But, no matter. By the time they were done, Rachel felt victorious and she let out another triumphant exclamation.

Lou pulled off her gear and laughed. "Enjoyed that, did you?"

Breathlessly, Rachel bowed and said, "Yes, Sifu, very much."

"Good."

"I never expected to be able to hit you."

"You saw a weakness and you took advantage of it, which is what you're supposed to do. Besides, you being able to hit me makes me a better fighter."

"I don't understand."

"You just told me what my weaknesses are, so thank *you*." Lou bowed to Rachel in her gratitude.

"Oh. Never thought of it that way. You're welcome, I guess."

"Okay, I think that's enough for today."

"That's it?" Rachel wasn't sure about the reason for the short session. Did Lou think she was in a hurry to get back to Bobby? The truth was, she had enjoyed not thinking about him for the first time in days. She loved him beyond anything, but she had been so focused on him for the last several days that her own needs had fallen by the wayside and it was good to focus on something else for a change.

"Yes, we did what you needed to do today."

"What do you mean?"

Lou looked at Rachel squarely for a moment. "Rachel, what were you thinking about when you hit me?"

"Thinking about? I wasn't thinking much at all. I was too busy concentrating and trying not to get hit."

"Okay, let me ask a different question. How did it feel to be able to land a hit?"

"It felt pretty awesome, actually."

"When you came in today, were you angry?"

"At you? No."

"Not at me."

Lou didn't elaborate and finally Rachel understood and just nodded.

"And now?"

Rachel thought about it for a moment, and then a slow smile crept up. "Not as much. You're a sneaky wench, aren't you?"

Lou laughed. "I have my moments. As I said, we did what you needed to do today. Now go shower and then go tell that young man of yours about all the fun he missed out on."

Rachel was grinning now. "Yes, Sifu." She bowed, but remembered to stand her ground for Lou to exit first.

Chapter Twenty

Bobby was in the hospital a few more weeks. His doctors wanted to make sure that his recovery, both from his physical injuries and the ones that touched him more deeply, the ones only time and therapy would heal, had progressed enough that he didn't need constant care.

When he came home, Rachel moved in to take care of him. Chris put up no argument. When Rachel had to leave him to go to class, his mother would come by to make sure he got fed, despite his protests that he had a walking cast and one good arm.

It didn't take Bobby long to realize that Rachel's and his mother's need to take care of him was greater than his actual need to be taken care of, so he stopped protesting and just let it happen. The fact that his mother wanted to be a part of his life again was still hard for him to fully accept, but he knew it was a good step for all that.

His father also came by, sometimes with his mother, sometimes on his own. When he came alone they either sat in the living room and watched TV together or, sometimes, Howard brought a chessboard over, the same one he had taught Bobby to play on when Bobby was still awkwardly wearing dresses and going by a different name.

Father and son didn't feel the need to discuss anything and Bobby was just grateful for the company and the unspoken acceptance. One day while Bobby was staring at the board, trying to figure out his next move, Howard, who was sitting back in a kitchen chair and looking off into the distance with a small smile on his face, suddenly said, "That girlfriend of yours, she's something, isn't she?"

"Stop trying to distract me." Regardless, Bobby couldn't help the smile that escaped at the mention of Rachel.

"No, I was just saying—cute, smart, a fighter, loves you. You lucked out. Good job."

Never taking his eyes off the board, Bobby said, "As much as I appreciate the fact that you approve of my girlfriend, and I do, that isn't going to stop me from beating you." Then he moved a knight and captured his father's king. "Checkmate. Ha!" He looked up and grinned.

Howard studied the board thoughtfully. "Would you look at that? Huh." He sighed, and then laid his king on its side. "I guess you had to beat your old man eventually."

Bobby laughed. "Yep. Maybe next time you won't throw the game."

Howard looked offended. "Throw the game? You won that fair and square. And it's about time too."

"Okay, sure. I'll pretend you weren't taking pity on me."

"Son, I didn't take pity on you when you were eight. Why would I take pity on you now?"

"Okay, I'll believe you. And yes, my girlfriend is awesome, thank you for noticing."

"It's hard not to. She was by your side every day in the hospital. She kept a smile on her face every time she saw you, no matter how hard that was. She held up well. She loves you very much."

"I know."

"Son, I have never tried to tell you how to run your life so I'm not going to start now, but I will say this—if you let that one go, then you're not as smart as I always thought you were."

"I have no intention of letting her go."

"Good. Then don't screw it up."

Bobby laughed, but asked, "What do you mean?"

Howard sighed. "You have to be patient with her. Trust me, I'm an expert on that."

"Yeah, but what do you mean? Patient about what?"

"She's going to fuss over you for a while and probably treat you a little too delicately. It's all out of love, but don't snap at her when she does something for you that you really just want to do for yourself. She almost lost you and she's still dealing with that. Just give her time to get used to the fact that she didn't." Howard started to gather the pieces together and began to put them back in the box.

Bobby sat back in his chair and thought about what his father had said. His father said nothing more as he put the game away. Finally, Bobby said, "I understand. I'll be patient, I promise."

Father and son exchanged smiles and nods, and then Howard excused himself, saying he had to be getting home.

His father really knew what was going on in his head. Even though he had been home from the hospital for a few weeks now, Rachel still treated him like he was made of glass. It was one thing, he felt, to be cautious as he maneuvered around the house, but it was another to treat him that way in bed. She slept at his side and let him put his arm around her but she seemed afraid to even hug him. He understood it but he wanted his girl-friend back. Needed her, if truth be known.

That night as Rachel snuggled against him, he felt as if she was just barely there. She was lying on her side with her head on his good arm, her hand casually on his chest, but there was space between them that had never been there before the bashing.

"Rachel, I'm not going to break if you get closer to me, I promise."

"You're already broken," she said sadly.

Very gently he said, "Only on my left side. I want to feel you next to me, touching me."

"Okay." She snuggled closer, closing the gap between their bodies, even putting one leg over his like she used to.

"That's better."

"Yeah."

"This is way better than being in the hospital. At least now I'm not woken up at all hours."

"Oh, I could still do that if you want." Rachel raised herself up and grinned evilly at him.

"Only if you're going to be offering sexual favors. The nurses never did, no matter how often I asked."

"They didn't? You need better insurance."

"Tell me about it."

The conversation trickled away and Rachel snuggled even closer to him. Bobby nudged her head with his chin and she looked up at him questioningly, but then she seemed to understand.

She scooted her body up enough so that their lips could meet in a soft, slow kiss. She touched his cheek, then reached her hand around until it was behind his head, grabbing his hair. She changed position slightly so that she was practically on top of him and the kiss intensified. His hand found its way under her shirt, and he moaned against her.

She immediately stopped and pulled away. "Are you okay?"

"More than okay. Trust me, that was good. It was very good. I've missed you." He whispered, "Come back here. You were doing just fine."

"Good to see everything hasn't changed."

"Nope. I'm still the same horny teenage boy I was before I went into the hospital. Well, maybe more so now." He started to rub her back in a slow, sensual way.

"Aww, my poor deprived boy."

"Uh-huh."

She reached up and kissed him again, putting her hand under his shirt, then pulled his shirt up. She reached for his nipple, a place she hadn't ventured before. She looked into his eyes for confirmation that she could touch him there and saw him give her a slow nod. She scrunched down and lifted his shirt more until it was over his chest and she put her mouth to his nipple. She wanted to savor it, savor him. Slowly, she grazed her teeth over it and he groaned and shifted.

"Fuck!"

She chuckled to herself as she continued her work. She moved her right hand over to his other nipple and gave it a squeeze that made him arch his back and sharply inhale. With his free hand he pushed her head more tightly into him and her work on him came faster.

"Oh God, I want to push your hand down to touch me and I can't. Dammit!"

She pulled her mouth off his nipple long enough to chuckle and say, "I'll get there, just be patient," and then she went back to work. She was still delicate with him—she didn't want to hurt him—but that made their lovemaking all the more tender and sweet.

As the spring semester progressed, Bobby's casts came off, and with the help of Dr. Lou and a physical therapist his limbs were in proper working order again. His boss at the restaurant was nice enough to hold his job for him but Bobby had politely turned him down. Even though both times he had gotten jumped were unrelated to his job, the attacks had happened while he was working, and he still had some anxiety that he wasn't comfortable talking about yet. Marissa told him that her employer needed a janitor. That work appealed to him for its steady schedule, higher pay, and static location. He began working there in April and quite enjoyed it.

But he missed his singing. Plus, he'd been working on the lyric he had started months before. Even though it had originally started full of angst and anger, he was able to turn it into a positive song about independence. He was anxious for Rachel and his family to hear it. Chris was the only one in his family to have ever seen him perform, and he really wanted his parents to come. He called Al and had his name put on the roster for the next open mic.

On the night of the show, his parents sat at a table with Chris and Marissa, while Rachel sat at another with Dr. Lou. When Bobby took the stage, he looked over and winked at Rachel, who blew him a kiss and gave him a big smile.

As the applause died down, he approached the mic and said, "Thank you, thank you. Oh, it's good to be back on a stage. I've missed this. Did you miss me?"

He gave a cocky grin to the audience and they responded with more applause and a few whistles, one of which was from Rachel.

"Good. I got my parents here tonight, so be nice to me." The audience chuckled. "I also have the best girlfriend a guy could ever have. She supports me in everything I do and she was great at nursing me back to health. I would be remiss if I did not sing this first song for her."

He nodded to Rachel, and then the band started to play a soulful tune and he began to sing Kelly Clarkson's "Thankful." He closed his eyes through the more bluesy parts, with his hand to his chest, and swayed with the music. He made sure to make eye contact with Rachel again at the end and looked only at her as he finished the song.

The cheer that rose up when he finished was almost deafening. This time, Rachel didn't whistle or holler out—she seemed to be busy wiping her eyes. Dr. Lou did the whistling for her though, and Bobby, mic in hand, bowed to her from stage as he would have during training. With a wink and a smile, Dr. Lou returned the bow.

"Thank you all. Now for my next trick...I'm going to do something of my own. I hope you like it." He then went into his song, which he had entitled "It's About Me," a song about the push-pull relationship he'd been having with his mother. But in a larger sense, the song was about how sometimes parents just need to let their children go live their own life.

The lines he felt closest to were the repeated refrain, "It's about me, not about you, so shut your mouth and let me be." He had worried, at first, that it might sound a bit harsh and make his mother upset, which he really didn't want to do, considering how precarious their relationship was at the moment, but he had really written it for her and he wanted her to hear it. Needed her to hear it.

When the song was over and Bobby left the stage, his mother got up and went to him and said with tears in her eyes, "Letting you go is the hardest thing, so don't ask me to do that. But I will let you be. I'll let you be you. Oh..." She couldn't talk anymore, so she just threw her arms around his neck and hugged him.

Next, it was his father's turn. "I'm proud of you, son. That was pretty damn good."

Chris added, "Do you have to be the pretty one *and* the talented one?"

"But you're the...wait, which one are you again?" Bobby grinned.

"I'm the one who's going to raise your rent."

"Oh, the asshole, now I remember."

"We can share the title."

Lou leaned closer to Rachel and said, "Seems like a strange ritual they have."

Rachel looked incredulously at Lou. "Says the woman who called me a fool in Chinese."

Lou blushed. "Did I lie?"

"Beside the point."

"Never mind me, go congratulate that boy."

"Good idea." Rachel put her hand on Bobby's arm in order to get his attention away from his brother. "Excuse me, it's my turn." She put her arms around him and kissed him, though chastely, as his parents were watching. "That was awesome and I love you."

"Thank you and I love you too." He pulled her to him for a long hug and whispered in her ear, "Thank you, just thank you."

She squeezed him and buried her face in his chest, taking in his scent. Rachel sighed and stood there holding him, not caring about the others around them, just grateful.

CHAPTER TWENTY-ONE

In June, Rachel and Bobby went to Minnesota for Rory and Maggie's wedding, which the university had agreed to let them hold in the theater. Rory walked down the left aisle and Maggie the right, and then they came together in the middle and mounted the steps that had been placed there for that purpose. Rachel and Bill waited onstage to stand in attendance. All the members of the wedding party wore suits designed by Bill, so of course, they were fabulous.

Rachel wasn't used to wearing a suit and didn't feel totally comfortable in it, but Bobby told her repeatedly before the ceremony that she looked gorgeous. And she had to admit, Rory was beautiful and handsome at the same time. The silver suit shimmered on her and she looked like she was made for the suit, rather than the other way around.

Before the ceremony she and Rory were alone backstage.

"Wow, Morgan, you should wear these things more often. I say this without lust for once but damn, girl, you are fine!" She grinned.

Rory instantly blushed and began to straighten her already straight tie. "You think?"

"Oh, honey, if you had worn a suit a year ago things would have turned out way different for everyone."

"You say that as if you would have had a chance with me." Rory looked into the dressing room mirror and began to make little adjustments to her suit and her hair that didn't need to be made. Rachel went up to her, turned her to face her, and grabbed her hands.

"Stop that, you're already perfect. Maggie's going to melt when she sees you."

"Yeah?" Rory asked nervously.

"Yes."

"What about me? When I see her, I don't know if I'll be able to walk or remember what I'm supposed to say."

"Morgan, listen to me and stop freaking out." Rachel put her hands on Rory's shoulders and looked her in the eye. Rory returned the look, but her gaze was unsteady. "First of all, calm down. This is nothing. This will all be over in a few minutes, and then we get to the party. And you just have to stand there and look gorgeous and tell that woman you love her. If you forget your vows, just tell her that. That's all that matters. And if it helps, think of this as the best show you've ever done." She lightly slapped Rory on the cheek a couple of times and Rory smiled.

"I don't need any help with having rosy cheeks, thanks anyway. But you're right, nothing to it. People get married every day."

Rory took a deep breath and seemed to compose herself, but then she looked panicked again. She grabbed both of Rachel's arms. "Rachel, what if I'm not good at it?"

"Not good at what?"

"At being married? What if I can't adult? What if…what if I fail her?"

"Morgan, snap out of it. Don't make me smack you for real because I will. All I know about adulting is you have to do it whether you know what you're doing or not. You're going to get through it regardless. And you're not going to fail her. Now tie straight, boots on, and sally forth! The curtain is about to go up." Rachel had given Rory a similar pep talk the night their last show opened because Rory had been nervous that her voice would fail her.

Rachel took a step back and said loudly, "Places!"

That seemed to galvanize Rory into action and snap her out of her paralysis. She checked herself in the mirror one last time, took a deep breath, nodded to Rachel, and let Rachel leave first, since Rachel had to take her place onstage.

Now, onstage, Rachel watched as Rory and Maggie mounted the stairs hand in hand to the music of Louis Armstrong. She had to admit, Maggie also looked great. Maggie was wearing her hair down for the occasion and it looked stunning. The smile Maggie bestowed upon Rory really made her face beautiful.

Seeing Rory marry someone else didn't hurt nearly as bad as Rachel thought it would. She knew Rory was happy and in love and that it was returned. Her role as best person didn't require her to give away the bride, but Rachel realized that she could finally let Rory go, that it was time.

As Rory was saying her vows, Rachel kept stealing glances at Bobby, who was sitting in the front row beside Rory's parents. He looked so handsome, Rachel thought. They had gone shopping for his suit the previous week and it had been a wonderful thing to see the look of awestruck wonder on his face with each suit he tried on. As he had been checking himself out in the mirror, she kept thinking, *I'm in love with a boy and damn if he's not fine.* After they left the store she had barely been able to keep her hands off him, and he had teased her and called *her* the horny teenager.

Rory's fears did not come to pass—she made it through the ceremony without forgetting her lines. When it was over they lingered at the kiss and the audience laughed. Rachel looked at Bill and they both shrugged. Rory and Maggie were still kissing when Bill held out his arm to Rachel and they walked down the stairs together and down the right-hand aisle, out of the theater.

Rory and Maggie and the rest of the wedding party took their places in the receiving line; Bobby stood off to the side with Dix. Rory's parents were the first in line and they hugged everyone and gave their congratulations. Then came an older woman Rachel had never met before. She went up to Maggie and said, "I wish your father could have been here to give you away."

Maggie's lip trembled and Rory held fast to her hand. She said, "Me too, Mother, me too."

Mrs. Parks looked at Rory and said, "You look a little young to me but I guess that's all right. You treat her with respect, you hear me? Or I'll come all the way from Boston to give you a good thrashing."

"Yes, ma'am, you have my word."

"Margaret, I'll expect to see the two of you in Boston over the holidays. I understand you will have to split the holidays between me and her parents but we'll work it out in time."

"Yes, Mother, we will." Maggie wiped her eyes but stayed where she was, and her mother didn't move to put her arms around her and quickly moved on.

Rachel leaned into Rory and whispered, "What the hell just happened?"

Rory whispered back, "Maggie made up with her mother last semester when she went to Boston for that conference. They're on speaking terms again. What you just saw was a good thing."

"Oh, okay."

They adjourned to a private room in the campus cafeteria. It was there that Rachel was able to get a moment alone with Bobby. They sat together at a table in the corner, a piece of cake in front of each of them. Bobby devoured his and was eyeing hers. Grinning, she slid it over to him and he gave her a grateful smile.

"You know, I really like it here," Rachel said.

"Yeah, it's a pretty campus."

"And from what I hear, Minnesota's pretty awesome."

"Cold, I hear it's cold."

"Well, yeah, but still. I hear it's really liberal."

Bobby just shrugged as he concentrated on finishing her piece of cake.

Apropos of nothing, Rachel declared, "Bobby, I want to live here."

"What?"

"I'm out of school now and it's time I start thinking about my future." She had graduated the month before. "And I've been thinking a change would do us both good. There are theaters up here. Someone's bound to be looking for a dramaturge." She took his hand. "Would you consider moving with me?"

Bobby put down his fork and took her hand in both of his. "Rachel my entire family is in Illinois—"

"You're right, I shouldn't have asked. I'm sorry."

He continued as if he hadn't been interrupted. "My entire family is in Illinois, but so is a bunch of other shit I'd like to leave there. I can visit my family or they can visit me wherever I am, but a new start sounds awesome. I have no idea what I will do up here, besides freeze to death, but yeah, I'll come with you."

Rachel was surprised that he said yes so quickly, but she wasn't going to question it. Instead, she threw her arms around his neck and squealed. "Oh, yes! Thank you. I love you, Sweet Boy." She bestowed kisses all over his face and he couldn't help but laugh.

"Do I want to know what you're so happy about?" Rory had wandered over to Rachel and Bobby's table as she and Maggie were making their rounds around the room talking to all of their friends. Maggie, who had been in animated conversation with Bill and Dix, made her way to Rory's side and took her hand.

Rachel grinned up at Rory and said, "Guess who's relocating to Minnesota?"

Rory quipped, "Well, there goes the neighborhood."

"Oh, hush. Admit it, Morgan, you missed me."

Rory sighed in a defeated way. "Like I miss that mono I got in junior high when Steve Tompkins, who was infected and didn't know it, sneezed on me."

"Aww, you think of me as the kissing disease? You're sweet."

"More like the contagious part. But sure, let's go with what you said."

"Morgan, you make my heart flutter with love when you say things like that."

"Bobby, you do know what you're getting into right?" Rory quipped.

"I think so." He smiled at Rachel.

"Hmm. Well, good luck with that. Now, if you'll excuse me, I'm going to go make out with my wife." Rory put her arm around Maggie's waist and they started to walk away.

"I thought we were going to dance?" Maggie asked her with a smile.

"You say that like they're different."

Once they were gone, Rachel turned to Bobby and pointed to Rory and Maggie, who were now dancing to "Cheek to Cheek." "Relationship goals, innit?"

Bobby smiled at the newlyweds, then pushed his chair back and held out his hand. "Come on, let's go make out."

Rachel stood up and took his hand. "Bobby, they're just dancing."

Bobbie snickered. "That's what she said."

Rachel shook her head. "Teenage boy."

In a sing-songy way Bobby said, "You say dancing, I say romancing." He swayed from side to side and smiled at her.

"God, you're a dork." She sighed in happy defeat. "But also a very sweet boy. How can I refuse?"

"You can't." He grinned just as he had when he'd stood in her hallway with a warming bag in one hand and her receipt in the other. "Come on, Wild One." He pulled her to the center of the room and they began dancing cheek to cheek.

About the Author

T.L. Hayes is just your typical overeducated, underemployed dyke, in the process of starting new journeys. She has held many jobs, including customer service agent, housekeeper, and polltaker. None of them has been as satisfying as writing, especially writing stories with predominately gay characters. She holds master's degrees in English and educational studies, and an incredible amount of student loan debt. She has recently moved back to her home state of Illinois and is enjoying all four seasons again.

Books Available from Bold Strokes Books

A Lamentation of Swans by Valerie Bronwen. Ariel Montgomery returns to Sea Oats to try to save her broken marriage but soon finds herself also fighting to save her own life and catch a murderer. (978-1-62639-828-3)

Freedom to Love by Ronica Black. What happens when the woman who spent her lifetime worrying about caring for her family, finally finds the freedom to love without borders? (978-1-63555-001-6)

House of Fate by Barbara Ann Wright. Two women must throw off the lives they've known as a guardian and an assassin and save two rival houses before their secrets tear the galaxy apart. (978-1-62639-780-4)

Planning for Love by Erin Dutton. Could true love be the one thing that wedding coordinator Faith McKenna didn't plan for? (978-1-62639-954-9)

Sidebar by Carsen Taite. Judge Camille Avery and her clerk, attorney West Fallon, agree on little except their mutual attraction, but can their relationship and their careers survive a headline-grabbing case? (978-1-62639-752-1)

Sweet Boy and Wild One by T. L. Hayes. When Rachel Cole meets soulful singer Bobby Layton at an open mic, she is immediately in thrall. What she soon discovers will rock her world in ways she never imagined. (978-1-62639-963-1)

To Be Determined by Mardi Alexander and Laurie Eichler. Charlie Dickerson escapes her life in the US to rescue Australian wildlife with Pip Atkins, but can they save each other? (978-1-62639-946-4)

True Colors by Yolanda Wallace. Blogger Robby Rawlins plans to use First Daughter Taylor Crenshaw to get ahead, but she never planned on falling in love with her in the process. (978-1-62639-927-3)

Unexpected by Jenny Frame. When Dale McGuire falls for Rebecca Harper, the mother of the son she never knew she had, will Rebecca's troubled past stop them from making the family they both truly crave? (978-1-62639-942-6)

Canvas for Love by Charlotte Greene. When ghosts from Amelia's past threaten to undermine their relationship, Chloé must navigate the greatest romance of her life without losing sight of who she is. (978-1-62639-944-0)

Heart Stop by Radclyffe. Two women, one with a damaged body, the other a damaged spirit, challenge each other to dare to live again. (978-1-62639-899-3)

Repercussions by Jessica L. Webb. Someone planted information in Edie Black's brain and now they want it back, but with the protection of shy former soldier Skye Kenny, Edie has a chance at life and love. (978-1-62639-925-9)

Spark by Catherine Friend. Jamie's life is turned upside down when her consciousness travels back to 1560 and lands in the body of one of Queen Elizabeth I's ladies-in-waiting…or has she totally lost her grip on reality? (978-1-62639-930-3)

Taking Sides by Kathleen Knowles. When passion and politics collide, can love survive? (978-1-62639-876-4)

Thorns of the Past by Gun Brooke. Former cop Darcy Flynn's heart broke when her career on the force ended in disgrace, but perhaps saving Sabrina Hawk's life will mend it in more ways than one. (978-1-62639-857-3)

You Make Me Tremble by Karis Walsh. Seismologist Casey Radnor comes to the San Juan Islands to study an earthquake but finds her heart shaken by passion when she meets animal rescuer Iris Mallery. (978-1-62639-901-3)

Complications by MJ Williamz. Two women battle for the heart of one. (978-1-62639-769-9)

Crossing the Wide Forever by Missouri Vaun. As Cody Walsh and Lillie Ellis face the perils of the untamed West, they discover that love's uncharted frontier isn't for the weak in spirit or the faint of heart. (978-1-62639-851-1)

Fake It Till You Make It by M. Ullrich. Lies will lead to trouble, but can they lead to love? (978-1-62639-923-5)

Girls Next Door by Sandy Lowe and Stacia Seaman eds.. Bestselling romance authors tell it from the heart—sexy, romantic stories of falling for the girls next door. (978-1-62639-916-7)

Pursuit by Jackie D. The pursuit of the most dangerous terrorist in America will crack the lines of friendship and love, and not everyone will make it out under the weight of duty and service. (978-1-62639-903-7)

Shameless by Brit Ryder. Confident Emery Pearson knows exactly what she's looking for in a no-strings-attached hookup, but can a spontaneous interlude open her heart to more? (978-1-63555-006-1)

The Practitioner by Ronica Black. Sometimes love comes calling whether you're ready for it or not. (978-1-62639-948-8)

Unlikely Match by Fiona Riley. When an ambitious PR exec and her super-rich coding geek-girl client fall in love, they learn that giving something up may be the only way to have everything. (978-1-62639-891-7)

Where Love Leads by Erin McKenzie. A high school counselor and the mom of her new student bond in support of the troubled girl, never expecting deeper feelings to emerge, testing the boundaries of their relationship. (978-1-62639-991-4)

Forsaken Trust by Meredith Doench. When four women are murdered, Agent Luce Hansen must regain trust in her most valuable investigative tool—herself—to catch the killer. (978-1-62639-737-8)

Her Best Friend's Sister by Meghan O'Brien. For fifteen years, Claire Barker has nursed a massive crush on her best friend's older sister. What happens when all her wildest fantasies come true? (978-1-62639-861-0)

Letter of the Law by Carsen Taite. Will federal prosecutor Bianca Cruz take a chance at love with horse breeder Jade Vargas, whose dark family ties threaten everything Bianca has worked to protect—including her child? (978-1-62639-750-7)

New Life by Jan Gayle. Trigena and Karrie are having a baby, but the stress of becoming a mother and the impact on their relationship might be too much for Trigena. (978-1-62639-878-8)

Royal Rebel by Jenny Frame. Charity director Lennox King sees through the party girl image Princess Roza has cultivated, but will Lennox's past indiscretions and Roza's responsibilities make their love impossible? (978-1-62639-893-1)

Unbroken by Donna K. Ford. When Kayla and Jackie, two women with every reason to reject Happy Ever After, fall in love, will they have the courage to overcome their pasts and rewrite their stories? (978-1-62639-921-1)

Where the Light Glows by Dena Blake. Mel Thomas doesn't realize just how unhappy she is in her marriage until she meets Izzy Calabrese. Will she have the courage to overcome her insecurities and follow her heart? (978-1-62639-958-7)

Escape in Time by Robyn Nyx. Working in the past is hell on your future. (978-1-62639-855-9)

Forget-Me-Not by Kris Bryant. Is love worth walking away from the only life you've ever dreamed of? (978-1-62639-865-8)

Highland Fling by Anna Larner. On vacation in the Scottish Highlands, Eve Eddison falls for the enigmatic forestry officer Moira Burns, despite Eve's best friend's campaign to convince her that Moira will break her heart. (978-1-62639-853-5)

Phoenix Rising by Rebecca Harwell. As Storm's Quarry faces invasion from a powerful neighbor, a mysterious newcomer with powers equal to Nadya's challenges everything she believes about herself and her future. (978-1-62639-913-6)

Soul Survivor by I. Beacham. Sam and Joey have given up on hope, but when fate brings them together it gives them a chance to change each other's life and make dreams come true. (978-1-62639-882-5)

Strawberry Summer by Melissa Brayden. When Margaret Beringer's first love Courtney Carrington returns to their small town, she must grapple with their troubled past and fight the temptation for a very delicious future. (978-1-62639-867-2)

The Girl on the Edge of Summer by J.M. Redmann. Micky Knight accepts two cases, but neither is the easy investigation it appears. The past is never past—and young girls lead complicated, even dangerous lives. (978-1-62639-687-6)

Unknown Horizons by CJ Birch. The moment Lieutenant Alison Ash steps aboard the Persephone, she knows her life will never be the same. (978-1-62639-938-9)

www.ingramcontent.com/pod-product-compliance
Lightning Source LLC
Chambersburg PA
CBHW030514020726
47494CB00004B/1087